MARIA MATIOS

HARDLY EVER
OTHERWISE

GLAGOSLAV PUBLICATIONS

...HARDLY EVER OTHERWISE
by Maria Matios

Originally published by Piramida Literary Agency
in 2007 in Ukraine as ...*Maizhe nikoly ne navpaky*

Translated from the Ukrainian by Yuri Tkacz

Ukrainian Copyright © Maria Matios, 2007
Cover art © Serhiy Ivanov

© 2012, Glagoslav Publications, United Kingdom

Glagoslav Publications Ltd
88-90 Hatton Garden
EC1N 8PN London
United Kingdom

www.glagoslav.com

ISBN: 978-9-491425-12-7
ISBN: 978-1-909156-34-0
ISBN: 978-1-909156-35-7

This book is in copyright. No part of this publication may be
reproduced, stored in a retrieval system or transmitted in any
form or by any means without the prior permission in writing of the publisher, nor be otherwise circulated in any form
of binding or cover other than that in which it is published
without a similar condition, including this condition, being
imposed on the subsequent purchaser.

MARIA MATIOS

HARDLY EVER
OTHERWISE

Translated from the Ukrainian
by Yuri Tkacz

GLAGOSLAV PUBLICATIONS

CONTENTS

FOREWORD

Maria Matios is currently one of the top women writers in Ukraine. Her novels reflect the wild spirit of the Hutsuls, highlanders from the Carpathian Mountains, whose remote villages still retain the old customs and colorful dress.

Herself born in the Carpathian Mountains, Maria bases many of her books on her family's unique experiences. She is a great fan of her native language. Her interests include psychology and ethnography. In literature she is a great martyr, a day-dreamer, a moderate adventurer and a lover of mystification. Maria loves to go about barefoot and grow flowers as she dreams up new plots for her novels.

Matios is the author of 7 collections of poetry and 14 books of prose. Her famous *Sweet Darusia* (2003) and *Nation* (2002) have each been reprinted four times. Several of her books have been published in translation in Poland, Russia and Australia. Excerpts of her works have been translated into German, French, Romanian, Slovak, Italian, Serbian, Czech and Hebrew. *Hardly Ever Otherwise*, together with *Sweet Darusia* and *Nation* have been made into popular plays. Her other recent titles include *Mamma Maritsa – The Wife of Christopher Columbus, The Russky Woman* (2008) and *Armageddon Has Already Happened* (2011).

In 2005 Maria Matios won the prestigious Shevchenko Literature prize. She lives and works in the Ukrainian capital Kyiv, but retires to the Carpathian Mountains for inspiration.

The cover art is by Serhiy Ivanov, an artist living and working in Lviv. He has illustrated many books and recently held a personal exhibition entitled "Hutsul Mythology".

I would like to thank Graham Hirst for editing the text, however the responsibility for any errors is all mine. Thank you also to my family for putting up with my absences while I translated the book.

Yuri Tkacz,
Translator of *Hardly Ever Otherwise*

PART ONE

FOUR BROTHERS,
LIKE KITH AND KIN

Odokiya, known as Dotsia to everyone at home, was the wife of Cheviuk's eldest son Pavlo. She was having such difficulty carrying her fourth child, that even her father-in-law Kyrylo, a soft-hearted man, but short on words, was forced to intervene in the matter, which in Tysova Rivnia was never considered delicate, insomuch as it was no one else's business.

From time immemorial women's pregnancy in these parts had been accepted as an everyday affair. Almost a secondary thing, one could say.

Since the beginning of mankind, men had been worrying about having healthy seed and women – an enduring womb. And that was the long and the short of it.

However, having watched Dotsia's daily vomiting around the stable and seeing his daughter-in-law waste away into ash after living for several months on apples and water, Kyrylo said to his wife Vasylyna one night:

"We have to do something about Dotsia."

There was firmness in Kyrylo's voice, which everyone in the house always heeded.

"What can I do?" Vasylyna asked, sitting up in bed and sleepily rolling her eyes upward. "I had trouble carrying Andriy as well, but did your departed mother take pity on me? My eyes were ready to pop out swinging that stupid hoe about while the child was ready to come into the Lord's world, and your mother only egged me on: 'Eh, let's do two more rows, and that'll suffice. You're not hoeing it properly, anyway.' 'So what's the proper way, mum?' I asked her. And she answered: 'Don't know, but that's not the right way.' That's what it was like for me. Have you forgotten that our Andriy was born in the pumpkin patch?"

"Stop nattering and contradicting me, woman! I haven't forgotten a thing. And leave my departed mother in peace! All her sins have been listed for her in the other world. Are you blind? Our daughter-in-law is fading before our eyes and won't utter a word of complaint. Look, we know that even if she gives birth to a cripple, it'll be no calamity: they'll manage to bring it up. But if Dotsia dies in childbirth, Pavlo will have to remarry. And he's already got three children. Who needs someone else's children to worry about? If his second wife bears him a child – the three he has now will become estranged from him. A stepmother is no sweet lollipop. Perhaps you've become so hardhearted toward Dotsia because you've forgotten what it's like being an orphan, eh?" Vasylyna heard out her husband's monologue through gritted teeth, although the silence was difficult to sustain.

When she lay back down beside Kyrylo, she found that sleep had abandoned her completely, because she was filled with anger. She wasn't too fond of her first daughter-in-law, solely because of one thing: the rock-hard, silent love of her eldest and kindest son, Pavlo, for his Dotsia.

Vasylyna had never seen Pavlo show great affection for his wife or ingratiate himself with her, even after he returned from the war. She had never seen him press her against the storehouse wall, for example, or roll about with her in the hayloft above the stables.

But the fact that her Pavlo was incapable of even breathing without Dotsia – this she knew intuitively.

To tell the truth... at least Vasylyna could admit to herself the number of times she had seen double and there had been ringing in her ears as she stood stock-still outside the door or the windows of the house where Pavlo and Dotsia were spending the night together unsupervised before they were married, in an effort to catch any sounds emanating from inside the walls. Above all Vasylyna wanted to relive at least one fleeting moment from her own past, the kind of moment which now appeared to her to have never taken place, a moment which only seemed like a mirage from her youthful years with Kyrylo.

However, Pavlo and Dotsia seemed to be so secretive, that the mother was left only with a profound anger and wordless astonishment when early in the morning her son and daughter-in-law took to work with such earnestness, as if they wanted to hurry the day toward evening, so that they could jump back into the steaming hot night together.

And there *was* something to remember…

But… perhaps only to remember. Because a sudden illness had taken Kyrylo's masculine strength from him, as if it had never existed. More than likely some two-legged she-devil had envied them their sons, healthy as nut kernels, and had ended the days of Vasylyna's pleasure, making Kyrylo impotent well before old age, an affliction worse than being crippled.

What could she do? It was fate! Kyrylo's father had given his mistress a child at seventy-five years of age, while here…

And so Vasylyna had secretly resented her daughter-in-law almost from the very start for enjoying with Pavlo what she had long since forgotten.

Who could she talk to about this?

Vasylyna knew only too well that in character and virility Pavlo was like the old Kyrylo, who now only lazily played with her occasionally, when they returned from some celebration, unlike in days gone by when he had taken no notice of Lent or Easter, or even a death next door. That's how it had once been, but now all that had changed...

Meanwhile Pavlo was making Dotsia children. And he did this without using carrots. The proper way.

...And so, having sighed a thousand times from self pity for her predicament and out of anger toward Dotsia, Vasylyna went off to the sorceresses and herbalists, just as Kyrylo had bade her, to seek help for her daughter-in-law. In their family a wife had no right to disregard her husband's bidding.

However, neither herbs nor church services helped Dotsia: she simply faded before everyone's eyes, except that her recently-sunken stomach began to swell, as if it was feeding on yeast.

'There's surely a cripple growing in her belly. Holy saints above!' Vasylyna crossed herself wordlessly, watching as her daughter-in-law finished tying the laces on her *postoly*[1] with great difficulty.

"...WIFE, SUMMON ALL OUR CHILDREN FOR TOMORROW," Kyrylo commanded Vasylyna, after eating dinner in silence and saying grace.

"All of them?" asked Vasylyna, clapping her hands, and then for some reason wiping them on her apron.

"All of them!"

Vasylyna wept silently: 'Oh, all of them... You can't summon Dmytryk from the grave... So Kyrylo has dreamed up some plan. God in Heaven, protect everyone's children and our own...'

Cheviuk's three sons, Pavlo, Andriy and Oksentiy, identical as three drops of water, sat around the oak table

---

1 *Postoly* – moccasin-like shoes worn by the Hutsuls, Ukrainian highlanders from the Carpathian Mountains in southwestern Ukraine.

in the middle of the largest room, which was usually re-served for guests. The fourth drop of this same water, the father, paced in silence around them, pausing for a long time behind each son's back and briefly slapping each on the neck.

Kyrylo was silent, because he was thinking; the sons sat silently, because they did not know what their father was thinking.

"Let's pray for Dmytryk…" he finally said.

All four of them turned their eyes toward an icon of the Holy Virgin under an embroidered sash in the centre of the wall and held their palms together in prayer.

"…Accept, oh Lord, the sinful soul of your servant Dmytro into Your Heavenly Kingdom, and shield us from evil intent and foolish actions…" the old Cheviuk finished the prayer with some unusual words and as-sumed his place at the head of the table.

Andriy and Oksentiy seemed to clear their throats.

Only Pavlo wiped a tear from his eye.

AFTER HIS HORRIFYING DEATH no one had spoken of Dmytryk in the Cheviuk household.

They simply prayed.

There was nothing to say.

Those who knew crossed themselves in silence.

Whilst those who were not privy to the details of the dark story made no attempt to ask any questions.

Kyrylo was in essence a kind and gentle soul, but he would have killed anyone with his bare hands had they dared mouth off against his youngest son, whom they had buried as a single man in the cold clay, before he had even celebrated his twentieth birthday.

No one knew, however, that Kyrylo was ready to forfeit everything he owned just to find out the name of the animal that had killed his innocent child.

...What had happened to Dmytryk Cheviuk habitually happened to people not only in times of war, but in any old year and during any season, when one half of the material world was choking on misfortune, and the other half thirsted for adventure.

It was the same old thing in this world: one set of people killed other people, and at this same time another set of people loved yet others. And yet others hated those who had loved.

And neither the first lot, nor the second lot could cope.

Either with the love.

Or the hate.

And hardly ever was it otherwise.

...*WHEN IVAN VARVARCHUK*, like many men from Tysova Rivnia, was taken away to fight for Emperor Franz-Josef, his young wife Petrunia was left all alone with a fair-sized estate to look after. Sometimes she managed well, and at other times she was barely able to cope looking after her burgeoning landholding.

But when in the space of a single week in the Varvarchuk's farmyard two cows calved, a mare foaled, the sow had ten piglets, the yearling bull began to snort through his inflamed nostrils, like a bear in the brambles, and to hoof the stable floor so forcefully that sparks flew out from under the floorboards, and the leg of the wife herself was bitten by a weasel, Petrunia convinced her nearest neighbours to allow their youngest lad to give her a helping hand, not as a hired labourer, but merely to help out.

The Cheviuks had never been poor, so they never hired their children out as labourers.

But they took pity on Petrunia, as a neighbour: after all, their own eldest son Pavlo, like her Ivan, was fighting at the front for the Kaiser.

The agreement between Kyrylo and Petrunia was a simple one: Dmytryk would look after the Varvarchuk's cattle, and in return the meadow hay and two mowings of late-season hay from Pohar together with two *kopy*[2] of maize from Varvarchuk's garden in Trepit would go to the Cheviuks, in lieu of payment for their helper Dmytryk.

Quiet and hard-working Dmytryk, from whom no one ever heard an unnecessary word, cleaned out the cow stalls and tended to the mangers from morning till night, without so much as putting down his pitchfork, shovel or cattle brush. Even the Varvarchuks' bull, fierce as a proper Epiphany frost, began to rub against Dmytryk's shoulder almost trustfully, and stopped overreacting at the appearance of strangers in the yard.

Everything would probably have remained so peaceful and good to this day, had not the farmer's wife clambered up onto the loft in the stable one autumn afternoon to fetch some hay for the calves.

And Dmytryk, who had been feeding a cow from a bucket, at that very moment happened to glance up, without first closing fast his innocent but all-seeing eyes, the eyes of a virgin…

---

2 1 *kopa* = 60 sheaves. A sheaf is a bundle of unthreshed corn tied with string.

The hay in the stables crumbled well even in winter, when it was trampled by ardent young bodies.

Even the hot breath from two mouths until recently speechless, but now rent apart by indescribable pleasure, rose up to the cold roof like smoke from a recently-lit fire.

And thus two people, both strangers only the day before, and now crazy from the sudden fire in their blood, easily and thoughtlessly lost their heads without the help of axes or gallows.

And thus when Andriy Cheviuk arrived unexpectedly one day at Petrunia's place, ostensibly to give his younger brother a hand, and found the door to the stable ajar, he did not think long: like a cat, he deftly sprang up the ladder leading to the loft.

After what he had seen, Andriy could barely stop himself from exclaiming "Oh my-y-y God!", which would have been natural in the circumstances.

But even if he had not restrained himself, no one would have heard him.

...*BLESS THE LORD, IVAN VARVARCHUK* found himself returning home from the war one fine spring day as fast as his feet could carry him, dust rising from his worn *postoly* and footcloths.

Cheviuk's second son, Andriy, met up with him outside the Jewish inn, apparently accidentally, as if he had long been waiting for the soldier to appear.

Obviously, he wanted to learn the truth about the war.

The small oil lamp, hanging up near the ceiling in the smoke-filled inn, glimmered lazily over the pair until the approach of midnight, illuminating a steadily increasing number of empty bottles between Andriy and Ivan.

15

However, while Andriy was unable to hold his tongue, Ivan's had become stuck fast to the roof of his toothless mouth.

And Ivan's feet, so healthy and swift in the morning, like those of a buck during rutting, had gone limp as the day unfolded, as if they were becoming increasingly paralyzed. Either they had lost all feeling due to the exhaustion of military duty the day before, or from the sudden languor of the present day, but in any case they wouldn't allow him to get up from the table. Perhaps because of what he had heard and drunk...

Tipping his hat twice before the innkeeper, Andriy backed off toward the old smoke-stained door. Ivan meanwhile ran his intoxicated eyes across the walls of the inn and held his head firmly in his hands, giving the impression that it was about to roll off his shoulders.

Varvarchuk would have remained sitting like this in the Jew's place until dawn, had the innkeeper's wife Fira not forcibly pushed the former rifleman outside, so that he would finally show himself at home:

"That's fine Ivanko, but you've returned from the war, not some hunting trip. So drag those feet of yours home, while it's still dark, while your wife's still tossing about in a warm bed," Fira told him, at the same time pushing him in the back. "You can show her your trophies tomorrow. My Leiba said he'll come round to see them too..."

At home Ivan did not tie Petrunia down to the bench with her plaits, nor did he grab the whip. True, he didn't try to be intimate with his wife either, until he was satisfied that her belly was empty and that there was no hint of the presence of another man either in the house or under her skirt.

Ivan invited Kyrylo Cheviuk in for a drink as a gesture of thanks and good will, and, in parting, gave him a pair of Austrian binoculars nicked by a bullet in distant Serbia.

And later, in the summer, for the feast of Kupalo[3], Varvarchuk invited over the two Cheviuks, Andriy and Dmytryk, together with his wartime friend Hryhoriy Keyvan – otherwise known as Hrytsko, to celebrate the festival of the church's patron saint.

For some reason Dmytryk was not very eager to come along to the celebration, but he did not dare stay away either. However, wonder of wonders, Andriy seemed to puff out visibly at the invitation, just as a cow's udder distends with milk in the last months of being with calf.

But there was no festive atmosphere in the house.

Petrunia moved about with lowered eyes between the oven and the table, like a poisoned mouse in the storehouse. She seemed exhausted, famished.

The men did not engage in any particular conversation, chatting a little about the war, and more about the current year's wet summer and minimal hopes for increases in stock numbers.

Dmytryk sat silently, watching either Andriy or Petrunia, as if he hadn't seen enough of them prior to this.

A little later Andriy somewhat uncertainly left the house, without uttering a word, as if leaving to relieve himself, but instead he snooped around the house and, having surveyed the street, stood on guard at the gate.

Ivan, after taking a quick look outside as well, locked the house from the inside with two yew-wood bolts. Then he raised the wilted Petrunia's arms and without uttering a single word tied her up to the clothes rack near the ceiling, shoving a rag into her mouth.

---

3   That is, on 24 June.

And only after this did the military comrades set about their planned work.

Hrytsko, just as silent, bound the docile Dmytryk's hands and feet with horse reins, and lay him down on the ground, pressing with his shoe against the lad's chest.

Meanwhile Ivan pulled out some planks from under the bed, which had been set aside for a new ceiling. For some reason he stroked each board with his hands, as if he was stroking a living person. Then he placed them one on top of the other in the middle of the room.

Next the two men, again saying nothing, took Dmytryk by the hands and feet and stretched him out on top of the boards; face down, so that he could breathe more easily.

Only after this did Ivan place the two widest, but thinnest boards, on top of the lad.

And only after this did the two men take off their shoes…

They jumped about on top of poor Dmytryk, as if they were dancing the wild *hutsulka* dance, stopping only after they heard that his bones no longer cracked and the lad had stopped rattling.

And at night they took him away by horse to the outskirts of the village and left him on the rocks, where the water from the mill fell with a roar.

… *SPREADEAGLED IN THE WATER, DMYTRYK'S BODY* was found near the Jewish mill by his own brother Andriy, who happened to be returning home toward morning after spending the night with some vivacious married woman in a nearby village.

And so he carried his unconscious brother back to their father's house.

However, the youngest Cheviuk did not cough up his mashed-up innards in his parents' home, but on the oven of his brother Pavlo. And for two autumns and winters Dotska, biting her lips with pity, changed the fresh pig's membrane on Dmytryk's chest and shoulders, fed him hot milk with badger fat and roseroot, and rubbed his yellowing skin with herbal creams and arnica oil.

Neither straight away, nor later, nor at any time at all did Dmytryk say a word about his ordeal either to his dad, or his mum, or to Pavlo himself, who adamantly refused to let his baby brother be looked after even by his parents. Pavlo had undertaken to care for his brother until death, even if Dmytryk were to live to a hundred.

Fate, however, entertained no thoughts of allowing Dmytryk to live so long, and probably had never intended to. It did prescribe him Christ's suffering. Occasionally, those who came around to sit with Dmytryk, to chat to him and sigh deeply later on their own, begged the Lord to grant him death, as one would ask for good health or happiness.

Dmytryk never spoke to his visitors.

He only listened.

Or else he might nod his head and wriggle his yellow fingers. But when the visitor said uncertainly in farewell "Good health to you!" – Dmytryk summoned all his strength and answered in a barely audible voice: "Come in good health… Dmytryk will be waiting for you."

For days he would keep his eyes peeled to the door. As if waiting for his salvation to appear. Sometimes he would stretch out his neck like a turkey in order to catch a glimpse of the top of the tree visible through the window or the tip of the neighbour's fence.

At times he wanted to talk. In the evenings – with Pavlo. During the day – with Dotska. But then he could remain silent for weeks on end and merely stared at the door, or pierced the ceiling with his eyes.

However, if ever the second born son, Andriy, visited the house, Dmytryk would always turn his head and his whole body, if he could, toward the wall no matter how difficult he found it, pretending to be asleep or dozing. And he did this in such a way that no one apart from Dotska realized that the brothers had not exchanged a single word in two years.

Then one day when Andriy crossed the threshold of Pavlo's house, Dmytryk was unable to even turn his head away.

And Dotska realized that the lad was ready to die.

No sooner had the door closed after Andriy, than she covered the windows with linen cloth, chased the children outside, locked the house from the inside, steeped some fragrant late-season hay in boiling water and with a small wad of young, very soft wool, began to wash Dmytryk's pain-racked body, clenching her teeth so hard, that it seemed in a short while her white teeth would disintegrate into dust.

Dmytryk looked at her in silence for a long time with his kind, large brown eyes, and the tears involuntarily ran down his face.

He had long since stopped being ashamed of lying naked before his sister-in-law. And this time he seemed to let her wash his desiccated skin even more subserviently.

If Dmytryk hadn't forgotten how to speak in all this time, it was only due to Dotsia's efforts.

But no one knew anything about this.

"Don't wash me so nicely, as if I'm about to be wed. Forgive me, Lord, but I won't be confessing my sins. I don't dare tell even the priest the truth. Only maybe you, Dotska... Because you're kinder to me than my own mother..."

"*Yoy*, Dotska, Dotska! If only you knew what you don't know..."

He caught his breath, as if he had hoisted a boulder upon himself, and then shifted it from his shoulders:

"Caress that stupid fool of mine one final time, Dotska, since it's because of him that I have to die..." Dmytryk asked of his sister-in-law suddenly, like a small child.

Then with the bare bones of his right hand he grabbed her hot palm and pulled it down past his belly. His belly seemed to have become stuck to his backbone.

If someone had ever told Dotsia that she could have easily ventured to do such a thing – she would have pulled a large tuft of hair out of their head in public.

But ever so submissively Dotsia merely covered the spot, where Dmytryk had placed her hand.

She seemed to be bewitched today. It was as if some stranger had taken over her body and changed the former Dotska.

Now she could smell burning candles in the house.

And frankincense.

The tips of her fingers could already sense the yielding softness of the crumbly clay of the cemetery.

She already felt sick from the smell of fir resin on the funeral wreath and the freshly-planed cross in the entrance hall.

None of this existed yet, of course. But for a moment Dotsia closed her eyes – and the fresh smells of an imminent death became intermingled with the smells of Dmytryk's deteriorated body.

She was terrified.

And felt strange.

And morbid.

And there was no one to speak to.

And there was not even time to be alarmed.

For Dotsia had never before held in her hands a living person whose soul was departing for the heavens before her very eyes. But the soul was being released, as if there was no fear at all, in fact as if there was a desire to leave.

With all his might he was still trying to breathe, this poor little Dmytryk of hers, but the last drops of life were already seeping from his body.

He was uttering a proper death rattle that filled the house, the holy icons and probably Dotsia herself. The rattle in his chest was identical to the rattle inside the oven when beetroot-leaf meat rolls were left to slowly finish cooking in the dying embers.

And his blue lips looked like crushed plums.

Only Dmytryk's eyes, deeply set in their black sockets, still glimmered with a desire to live. But then this too was extinguished, just as glow-worms became extinguished in a forest at night when people deliberately stamped on them.

"Don't be afraid, Dotska… No one will punish you for this…" Dmytryk said softly.

Whether from the pain, or simply for no reason, he closed his sad eyes for a long time.

And then, perplexed, Dotsia fell with her wet face upon the sunken, but rough furrow shaved by her own hands along the yellow skin of Dmytryk's legs. The legs were thin as thin can be, the broken bones resembling cracked dry branches.

The bitter and powerless tears of a helpless woman fell upon Dmytryk's desiccated and blackened stump, emaciated like the rest of his body.

Even though she had two children of her own, Dotska had never seen a living male member in daylight, until she began looking after Dmytryk's crushed body.

Up until now they had seemed to exist separately. There was Pavlo's strong and healthy member, which she only felt inside her in ardent thrusts and pulsations of elastic male fluid. And then there was this wilted bud of Dmytryk's, which always lay benignly and indifferently before her eyes, perched between his broken legs when Dotska bathed or massaged the lad's wasting body.

Now, with dried chapped lips, she found herself whispering some kind of penitent prayer into that male shame of his (God Almighty!). She was inventing words as she went along, neither fearing nor feeling disgrace at her actions, at her brazenness, at Dmytryk's wide-open eyes, at his deep sighs and muffled sobs about something of his own, something secretive.

Slowly Dotsia washed Dmytryk with warm chamomile-infused water, without ceasing to caress his wrinkled skin.

This was no sin. A sin was not to grant the last wish of someone, who would no longer have any wishes the following day.

"I'll tell only you the truth, Dotska... Only you... I'm going into the clay because of Varvarchuk's Petrunia. We were lovers while Ivan was at the front. We loved each other so much, that...

And if you can, one day, tell Petrunia that I wouldn't have died for another woman, even if I had gnawed rocks

23

with my teeth. But as you can see, I'm willing to die for her.

... and beware of Andriy, Dotska. He was chasing Petrunia before she was married. And even after Ivan was conscripted into the army. But she let him have it between the eyes.

The Lord is my witness that I did not want to touch her... No, not quite... I wanted to, but not intentionally. I didn't know how. I knew that Ivan had gone off to war. That I shouldn't touch her. But when I saw her naked body on that ladder... Oh, Dotsia-a-a...

Andriy informed on me. He caught us one day in the hay. And Hrytsko Keyvan helped Ivan to crush me. Why? He's my godfather..!

Keep your hand there some more, Dotska. I won't harm anyone anymore. Not anyone.

But God forbid lest you tell any of this to father or Pavlo. I would damn you from the other world, if you were to do this. It's not Petrunia's fault. It's all because of her white body and my foolish head... let everyone think that I fell from the mill...

But when I remember, Dotska, how it was with her – I don't want to die, ever, although the Lord knows how much I am suffering.

But what of it, since I'm already dying...?"

"... *I'VE SUMMONED YOU, MY CHILDREN*, to let my will be known to you," Kyrylo said, running a heavy gaze over all three sons. "You are like three fingers on my hand. There used to be four, but that was a long time ago... and what of it now?!

I have no more than has been left to me. But you still have to provide for your families and maintain your farms.

We have acquired some things in our lifetime and will acquire still more. That's why we work. But I want to let my will be known to you now, because anything can happen. You will listen to me and do as I bid. If you heed my words, you will all fare well."

Kyrylo inhaled deeply and exhaled just as heavily:

"Pavlo and Odokiya will care for mother and myself. To Pavlo I've bequeathed our house, five *falchi*[4] of field in The Meadows and three *falchi* of pasture in The Hollow."

Oksentiy swallowed loudly.

Andriy scraped a finger across the tablecloth.

Pavlo placed both his hands before him.

"The three *falchi* of forest in Posich, which were to have been passed on to Dmytryk after he married," Kyrylo paused for a long time, as if struggling with a piece of something which had become lodged in his throat, "and Dmytryk's high plain in Kisny I've bequeathed to Andriy. The two of them were close from childhood, so I think Dmytryk will be asking from the other world for the Lord to intercede on your behalf, Andriy."

Kyrylo got up from the table and went over to the window. He pushed aside the linen curtain and pressed his forehead against the glass pane.

Through the window he could see the hills, the most distant of which, rounded like a full moon, was dubbed Kisny, meaning "mowable", because the hay mown from it was lush and thick year in and year out. For a moment Kyrylo thought he saw a flock of white sheep rambling along the Kisny ridge. Jumping over anthills, a joyous Dmytryk chased after them, a whip in his hand and a reed pipe stuffed under his belt. Behind him, wagging its

---

4   A *falcha* (plural – *falchi*) is a unit of measurement of pasture or field, equals 204.5 x 63.9 m

black and white tail, ran their dog Havchyk[5].

Oh, Havchyk… After Dmytryk's death the dog had howled outside the Varvarchuk's stable for a week until some merciful soul had shot it.

"…Dmytryk will be asking from the other world for the Lord to intercede on your behalf, Andriy…" Kyrylo repeated for some reason, and returned to join his sons.

Oksentiy sat with his back pressed against the chair and his arms folded across his chest.

Andriy scratched the back of his neck.

Pavlo drummed the table with his fingers.

Kyrylo again studied each of his sons.

"I won't leave you empty-handed either, Oksentiy, even though you married against our will and even though your wife brings our family into disrepute because she rides the rivers with the raftsmen like a cart without a shaft. You've already got stock, a high plain and your own house. For the moment I'll give you two more pairs of oxen and three horses. Plus the summer stable in Vypchyn. You have the wherewithal to farm, but no! If only you had the desire! So go make yourself some children so that you'll have someone to look after and someone to appreciate your work!"

Pavlo looked at his father – and adjusted the clasp on his shirt sleeve.

Andriy smiled into the corner of his thin lips.

Oksentiy bit his lower lip until it bled.

"The Lord willing, in a month or so Pavlo will have a fourth mouth to feed. You, Andriy, put the children you have now in order and make yourself a few more. Because what are two girls in a house without a single boy?

---

5   Literally, Little Barker.

"And Oksentiy will give his Yelena a few good beatings and quickly give her one in the spot that itches so badly. What?" he addressed Oksentiy. "Are you incapable of placating her tempestuous nature, so that she stops defiling the family name? If only she did it on the sly, but no – the whole world has to know about it!"

"People lie about Yelena, dad!" Oksentiy practically shouted and jumped to his feet.

"Sit down and listen to your father!" he pressed down on his son's shoulder. "I'm not passing on old wives' tales! I'm telling you what I saw with my own two eyes! And I'm telling you in our family circle, not at the local inn. Think hard! There's no need to jump up. If you farm, like everyone else, I'll give you some more. I'm not about to die this very hour. But I've written up a will covering you all. Let it be. It's never too late to add to it."

And from under the tablecloth he pulled out a document for each of them, witnessed by the notary in Vyzhnytsia, outlining the division of his estate among his sons.

At first the three sons silently exchanged glances.

Then in silencewordlessly, almost simultaneously, they embraced their father's shoulders.

In the Cheviuk family words alone carried little weight.

...EVER SINCE DMYTRYK HAD PASSED AWAY Dotsia kept dreaming of fire, night after night, for years.

No matter whether she lay down exhausted from work, as good as dead, or turned away toward the wall after almost fainting from Pavlo's strong body, she still kept dreaming of the fire, no matter what! And such a bright red colour it was, splashed across the snow like blood from frozen guelder-rose berries. And with such long tongues of flame. With sharp tips. And so all-consuming. Never leaving an untouched spot anywhere!

27

Dotska covered her face with her hands, and those sharp tongues licked her body, which was cold with terror.

They reached into her bosom.

Grabbed hold of her hair.

And she fought off the fire the whole night long, as if it was an assailant. However, she neither cried out nor screamed, only beat off the flames with her bare hands. But she lacked the strength to overcome this fierce many-headed creature.

Dotska woke up exhausted, dripping with sweat and consumed with fear.

For a long time she was unable to comprehend where she was and what was happening to her, but slowly her memory returned.

A mouse monotonously scratched up above in the attic; another rolled walnuts about. By her side Pavlo was breathing evenly after a hard day's toil. And through an open door she could hear the children snorting from time to time, smacking their lips.

Quietly Dotska slipped out from under the woolen blanket and got a drink of water. There was a burning sensation in her chest, as if a fistful of insatiable fire had just been wrenched from there.

Dotska drank quickly, hungrily, as if she had never before had a drop of water in her mouth.

However, between each mouthful she did not forget to glance outside.

An other-worldly weariness and silence hung over Tysova Rivnia and over their warm home.

There was not a soul anywhere.

Not a breath of wind.

Not a single hoot from an owl.

No dogs barking.

Only as if a coldness was descending upon every-thing. No, not quite. It was as if death was breathing coldly somewhere nearby.

A sudden hot flush engulfed Dotska from head to foot and touched her under her bed-shirt with living, hot hands: from behind the wall of the summer kitchen – Holy Mother of God! – Dmytryk emerged in full view of her. It wasn't exactly Dmytryk, only his white shadow, like a bundle of spun yarn tattered by the wind, with washed-out features, on legs of broken sticks. And for some reason this almost formless and morbid shadow stretched out its arms toward his father's house.

The old Cheviuks lived across the road to Pavlo. And Dotsia could plainly see a ball of fire rolling down her father-in-law's tin roof and landing at Dmytryk's feet. And just as suddenly flames engulfed the white locks of his long hair, grown out after years in the grave. Dmytryk was all white, like a beggar outside church at Easter. And he was covered in burning hot flames. He raised his arms to the heavens, and it seemed to her that she could hear the rustle of the flames from under his burning clothes.

Just as she was standing, Dotsia fell to her knees be-fore the icon in the corner, tightly clasped her eyes shut and began to recite prayers almost out loud. Her lips supplicated, one prayer after another, for the dead, the living and the unborn, and for those whom no one re-membered, and for those who had died from thunder or tempest, and for those who had sinned, stolen, lied or failed to forgive…

But Dmytryk did not disappear even when her eyes were shut. Now he was pointing at the fire surrounding his father's house, and yelling for Dotsia to come and help.

Dotsia could clearly hear Dmytryk's voice, but was unable to make out his words. He was becoming angry at her, almost trying to drag her to the fire. Andriy and Oksentiy dashed out unharmed from the fierce flames consuming their father's house and joyously began to squat dance around Dmytryk, who was engulfed in flames.

Everything was so alive, so real, as if it was happening before her eyes – she only had to reach out.

Dotsia again hurriedly crossed herself, trying to stop her knees from knocking together, and fearfully dived back under the woolen blanket, clasping her eyes tightly shut. And there Pavlo's roaming hand sleepily made its way into her fear-inflamed bosom.

…When the second roosters crowed, Dotska dreamt she was catching trout fry in a dam built with Pavlo's own hands somewhere in their orchard, which teemed with pesky bees and white cherry blossom.

At first she didn't understand that the rooster was telling her to wake up, reminding her that it was time to start work.

All day long Dotska so craved after that unfinished dream, that on the following night she dreamt of the fish again. But she was no longer scared. Neither of the fire, nor of Dmytryk. She knew that soon she would be pregnant.

When women dreamt of fish it meant a child was on the way. But her fourth pregnancy was like Christ's suffering: Dotska could eat nothing, apart from apples and water. She felt nauseous, even when she merely looked at people.

Few in Tysova Rivnia could recall such an amazing thing happening to a woman who was pregnant with a second or subsequent child.

VASYLYNA CHEVIUK EMERGED FROM HER HOUSE and set off for the fortune-teller while it was still dark. And she did well to do so. Because if you were lazy and got up after the second roosters had crowed, you would be late to give your feet some distance. And watch out, some misfortune was sure to cross your path: a slut, a widow, a woman of illegitimate birth or a she-devil. And you may as well head back home then, for all kinds of people can cross your path and bring you bad luck.

From the crack of dawn such women dawdled about the village, just waiting for the opportunity to cross someone's path, because something was troubling them. They carried empty pails and wore their skirts inside-out.

Now if Vasylyna were to chance upon Marynka-Godspirit, she need not have worried any more about her daughter-in-law's pregnancy.

Marynka was a sacred soul. She had died twice for no clear reason and each time the Lord had refused to accept her soul. Maybe she had wanted to do herself some harm, or perhaps it was only the gossips spreading scandal about her...

Pious Marynka went about the world with hands folded in prayer – letting everyone get on with their lives. And she didn't lecture anyone how they should live their life. She had wandered about until her hair had turned grey.

And the people rejoiced or were envious that such miracles should occur in God's own world. Which is why they called her "godspirit" – the Lord was not yet ready to accept her spirit.

Marynka was definitely a good person to come across. Sometimes she even stood watch to make sure no one bad crossed a person's path. If she uttered a kind

31

word after someone had passed, it was a guarantee that everything would be fine.

"How did you sleep, Vasylyna dear?!" Bandy-Legged Duck asked old Cheviuk's wife in a singsong, interrupting her lazy thoughts.

Even in the twilight old Cheviuk's wife felt as if someone had thrown a handful of salt into her eyes.

"All right. And you… Tsiutka?" Taken by surprise Vasylyna barely restrained herself from maliciously calling her namesake a Duck. However, she addressed her by the name that every Vasiuta in the village was called from a tender age – Tsiutka, an abbreviated form of "Vasiutka".

Old Cheviuk's wife imagined spitting over her left shoulder: 'May the devil take her away! No luck today! I may as well turn back!'

Everyone in the village knew that from birth the bow-legged Vasylyna, whom people openly called Bandy-Legged Duck, possessed a power somewhat greater than just simple fortune-telling. And so they tried to avoid finding their way onto her tongue and, even more so, tried not to appear before her eyes. No one had heard anything good about old Duck's abilities.

Meanwhile Tsiutka drew up to old Cheviuk's wife in the darkness and grabbed her right elbow with her left hand:

"Who knows why you're dashing about here at night, Vasylyna dear, when there's fire already swirling about your house?! Don't act so cozy. Don't kid yourself that you're rich! The rich have never been chummy with the Lord."

And she went off into the darkness like a ghost, without so much as a 'God be with you', her full skirt billowing in all directions, almost like that of a Gypsy woman.

"May you be sucked into the mud for blabbing such stupid things!" old Cheviuk's wife spat after her... and headed back home.

And that day Dotska felt the first kick of the child in her belly. And she finally felt better. Without needing the services of a fortune-teller.

... *ON THURSDAY MORNING* Kyrylo told Vasylyna to 'get everything ready'.

This meant that before the crack of dawn on the night of Thursday going onto Friday Cheviuk and his sons would set off hunting.

After such an order Vasylyna knew her work by heart: for Friday's meal – a meatless day – she placed a *garchyk*, a small wooden barrel with a deer carved into the handle, into a backpack made of thick leather. And she filled the *garchyk* with sauerkraut and honey-agaric mushrooms.

Then she baked a Lenten *malay*, a round cornmeal bread,

boiled some *banduli* – large white beans the size of half a pinkie – and dressed them with onions fried in oil.

And as for Saturday's meal, she never had any misgivings:

a large piece of yellowed salted fatback bacon from the previous year, two to three heads of freshly-pulled summer garlic, two fist-sized *brynza* sheep cheeses, a boiled-potato *kulesha*, and two dozen raw potatoes.

That would suffice.

Hunting was, for the Cheviuks, a very profitable affair: they were never short of meat. Some in the village were able to put meat on the table only at Christmas and Easter, but Vasylyna's grandchildren had to refrain from eating smoked hams perhaps only during the longest Lenten fast. The men never set off just to shoot hares. They always went for bigger game: when they cut short the life of a wild boar by putting a bullet in its snout, there was enough of that firm meat and bacon to keep the household going for well over a month.

Cheviuk's old wife had her own secret association with wild pigs. Most of all, especially during the fiercest of cold winters, she loved to prowl about the bedroom with the floor covered in coarse boar skins.

She loved listening to the crackle of burning logs in the oven.

Loved to see the tongues of the hobbled flames emerge through holes in the top of the stove.

To breath in the delicious smoke of the beech-wood logs.

Softly, almost on tip-toe, Vasylyna made her way to bed, continually stopping, while the coarse, untrimmed bristles of the pigskin sharply pricked her bare soles.

For a moment she closed her eyes and imagined that it was young unshaven Kyrylo back home from his job at the wood-mill in Shepit, who, unable to wait till evening, had dragged her into the hayloft above the stables, digging his prickly face and his hungry body into Vasylyna's equally hungry flesh... There was no time for a man to shave, if for a week or sometimes even two he had not savoured the smell of a woman beside him! Oh... It was great!

But it was great too when the hunters from their household chopped off a pair of deer antlers for her and brought back some young meat from the hunt to smoke! Then it was like Easter for Vasylyna. She could make all manner of things from forest goat or deer by salting, marinating or frying.

Heh! Deer meat was quite different to coarse pork. Deer meat required a delicate touch. If you held it over the fire too long or let it absorb too much smoke, you might as well give it away to the poor for a mere "God bless you". And how amazing was the taste of red, almost beetroot-coloured *buzhenyna* made from a year old deer!

The Cheviuks kept the *buzhenyna* tied up high on the beams near the ceiling in the store room, reserving it for festive days or honoured guests, out of reach of the children, so that they wouldn't grab themselves a piece whenever they pleased.

Vasylyna didn't even try to avert her husband from going hunting; in fact, she encouraged him. Other wives tried to dissuade their husbands from taking out their rifles, but not her. On the contrary, the evening before she would make love to her husband, caress him all over so that he would have a good heart when he had a weapon behind his back, and she saw him off into the pre-dawn cold.

The fortune-tellers from Rivnia narrated all kinds of foolish things about people who enjoyed hunting. For example, that in old age a hunter died a long and difficult death, just like his quarry. Or else that after he died, his body would ooze lymph, just as the wild game had bled blood, and that the body would become so bloated, it wouldn't fit into a coffin.

Oh the things envious people thought up when a hard-working husband returned from a hunt with a cart rolling behind him bearing a dead boar, a bear or a goat. On the floor of the cart, heavy with prey, yesterday's enemies lay peacefully side by side. The short and forever frightened tails of the hares next to the once proud tails of the bustard, grouse or woodcock, alongside the faded feathers of a kite or a grey partridge which now tickled the cooled heels of such royal quarry as wild cat, wolf or badger. And the yellow muzzles of the foxes bared their black teeth one last time at the heavens pregnant with clouds, beside the glazed blood-soaked eye of a falcon, majestic only yesterday, or the insolent stare of a hawk.

Finally all these treasures, until recently alive and fleet-footed, but now piled neatly and sumptuously upon the cart, accompanied by the tired but somewhat as-suaged hunters, slowly, almost lazily entered the Chevi-uks' yard.

Vasylyna first liked to bend over the game, to rest her gaze for a protracted time on the luxuriant but now indif-ferent beauty of these former rulers of the forest, subdued forever by lead shot. She would stand there a while, staring at them, perhaps throwing a still-hot fox tail over her shoul-ders, pinching at an owl's crest or tweaking a horned owl's beak, stroking a hazel-grouse with her eyes. All the while she'd be thinking how good it was to be human, rather than an animal, whose life could be ended at any moment – and only then did she set about her woman's work.

...KYRYLO INHERITED HIS LOVE OF HUNTING from his now deceased father, to whom the wild game came of its own free will, as they used to say in Tysova Rivnia, so that he had no need to go out and pursue it. To this day they tell tall stories of his various exploits, but one of these is mentioned more often than the others.

For Ananiy Cheviuk, Kyrylo's father, was an amazing hunter renowned throughout the region, perhaps even further afield.

Even under the former Austrian Empire during the annual hunt by the Kaiser's family in Berhometon-Siret[6],

6 Berehomet (until 1946 – Berhomet-on-Siret) is a large village located in the south-western part of Chernivtsi Province, in the beautiful foothills of the

his highness the heir to the throne, Franz-Ferdinand, had asked after Vasylyna's father-in-law, who was astonished by the sudden royal invitation and the inordinate attention lavished upon him. How was it that the subject of his highness, mister Cheviuk, knew how to hunt bear – without ever missing, without ever having been wounded and never emerging from the forest empty-handed?

In honour of the unprecedented occasion Ananiy was dressed in a long white shirt that was let out over white linen pants and a *keptar*[7] edged in thick fur on the ends of the sleeves. Holding a green hat, which he had prudently removed in front of the illustrious nobleman, he did not mull over his answer too long:

"If you please, sir, our Bukovynian uncle of a bear doesn't like red-hot fir trees."

"How do you mean?" the Kaiser's son asked in amazement.

"Exactly that!" Ananiy looked the wide-eyed nobleman straight in the eye. "He doesn't like them, and that's that! And I know this, so I take advantage of it. I hew a sharp stake from the trunk of a fir tree, make it burning-hot over the flames, and then steal up to the uncle. And to my inquiry: 'How was your day, sir?', uncle bear answers: 'Good health to you!' once and forever. The main thing is to aim well at the right spot."

"And where is the right spot?" smiled Franz-Ferdinand, eyeing his entourage, which had gone silent, nodding their heads in time to the Hutsul's account, as if confirming the veracity of his words.

Carpathian Mountains, on the banks of the swift-flowing Velyky Siret River. The name derives from the Ukrainian word *berehomet* – a place where the riverbank is washed by water.

7 *Keptar* – a sleeveless jacket made of sheepskin and ornately embroidered, worn by Ukrainian highlanders, the Hutsuls.

"Oh, your lordship... if you would be so kind... I can only show you. I wouldn't be able to explain it even to you," replied the cunning Ananiy, reveling in his momentary superiority over the heir to the throne. It transpired that there were things that even emperor's sons did not know, and the simple Ananiy had one over them. "I can take you along with me to Burchiv during the hunting season. There the uncles get about underfoot; sometimes they even get in the way."

"Do you ever entice uncle with dead game?" the Kaiser's son continued to question him unhurriedly. Himself forever embroiled in work, the old Ananiy envied the languidness of the heir to the throne. "You don't fool him by setting out a dead nag or a yearling lamb, do you? Placing its skinned carcass under a tree, climbing into the tree yourself, and then emptying your rifle into him – and no more *misha*?"

"Your Excellency..." Ananiy gazed at the young prince for a long time, as if deciding whether to convey to him the thoughts of an old hunter. However, after hesitating a moment longer, he said softly, but firmly: "I'd be a swindling old man if I were to fool a poor animal like that! Kind sir, Ananiy Cheviuk wants nothing to do with swindling. To clamber up a fir tree and shoot a deceived bear in the head is not a very difficult thing to do. But when you approach an uncle head on with a red-hot stake and look him in the eye – well that's quite another thing... Then it's either me, or uncle bear. So, forgive me, most noble lord..." Ananiy answered him, bowing low before his Excellency, and then pulled on his felt hat.

...The love of hunting was passed on from grandfather and father to Andriy.

Pavlo and Oksentiy were indifferent to hunting. But at their father's behest all four sons would clamber and crawl through mountains near and far, to return home exhausted and sated, one with adventures, another with impressions, a third with prey, and the eldest sated by everything at once.

And Vasylyna? Vasylyna felt good. Around their father even the older children acted as if they were small or at least different. Life was short. It was good for them to sit around a campfire at night in the forest, without any women, to talk man-to-man about life and ask their father for advice.

If only her daughters-in-law could be as sweet as her sons! But no, her sons' wives didn't act like daughters-in-law at all; hell knows what seed they had sprung from!

Dotska was like a rabbit, never able to satisfy herself with Pavlo. Always pregnant, having children. And Pavlo had to think how to feed those mouths.

True, her daughter-in-law had looked after Vasylyna's Dmytryk until his death. You couldn't say anything against her there. The truth is no lie.

But then she, Vasylyna, Dmytryk's mother!!! – wouldn't she have taken away the faeces from under him just the same, wouldn't she have also not been squeamish about washing his disgorged innards from the handkerchiefs, the way Dotska had done?!

Pavlo had become intractable, like never before, and for this reason it almost came to fisticuffs when the Cheviuks had begun to argue who would look after Dmytryk.

And Dmytryk, no matter how frail he was, said: "Dad... forgive me... forgive me this trespass, dad... But I'll go to die at Pavlo's place. And nowhere else."

Vasylyna could only clap her hands together upon hearing this, and later, more for the effect, she beat her head with her fists in public, repeating from time to time: "Oh, my bitter fate… why has such misfortune befallen us?"

Kyrylo loudly gnashed his teeth upon hearing Dmytryk's request, but did not dare refuse him.

And at night he struck Vasylyna several times in the back with his fists, something he had never done before:

"Why is your blood so bad, woman, that our son can sense it even before his death?"

But there was really nothing bad in her blood, except for the fact that she just plain didn't like Dotska. She simply didn't want her daughterin-law to take advantage of poor Dmytryk in his frailty. That was all that was bad in Vasylyna! That was why she dug her heels in when it came to Dmytryk being taken away by Pavlo. Her daughter-in-law might have added God only knows what to his food only to be rid of him sooner. How could Vasylyna have known how meticulously Dotsia would care after her unfortunate son?

But once Dotska began to deliberately care for Dmytryk, as if he were her own kith and kin, Vasylyna hated her older daughter-in-law all the more.

And Oksentiy's Yelena had caused her motherin-law even more angst. The slut. Her blood longed after other women's husbands. And when she was on heat, she would leave the farm and the children and sleep around with those who ran the rafts down the Cheremosh River. She lounged about until Oksentiy dragged her out of some tavern or from the home of another woman like herself and counted her ribs well with his whip, as if she were some thoroughbred animal.

However, Yelena's blood was settling in her veins too, probably, because she had at last borne Oksentiy three children in the past two years. And now she was looking to see if Kyrylo would change his mind and add some beech forest and land to the oxen and horses he had bequeathed them. Aha! Mum and dad had better things to do than to transfer title to their hard-earned assets to their barren seed. Let them wait a little longer! Vasylyna still needed the land herself. The best land was already Pavlo's. Kyrylo and Vasylyna would live their final days with Pavlo and Dotska, even though Dotska was a real pain in the neck.

And it was better not to even think about darling Andriy's woman. She had arrived with practically a bare backside and got all his wealth. What? With the cushions and blankets, the two heifers along with five pregnant ewes which Andriy's Nastunia had brought with her, how could you put in together to have a farm like other people's children?!

All the same, Vasylyna had convinced Kyrylo to bequeath to darling Andriy the assets which were to have gone to Dmytryk, the Lord rest his soul.

Darling Andriy was Vasylyna's little baby, the apple of her eye. He was the child of Vasylyna's foolish blood.

Pavlo, Oksentiy and Dmytryk were born just as they had been conceived: the usual way. What did a wedded wife need? To sleep well with her husband and bear him children. What else was there?

But no!

Something had come over Vasylyna when Andriyko was about to be conceived. She had raced about after Kyrylo like an untouched virgin. Despite already having two children, she felt heady, just as she had once felt in her youth after partaking of too much green poppy-head

41

juice in an effort to extinguish the pain of several days of toothache.

Oh, back then she had quelled her impatience for her husband's caresses wherever she could: in the pastures, in the sheep pens, in the maize fields, on the hay. She trembled like a leaf and spread out before him like mown grass. Kyrylo only needed to give her a sign, to squeeze his elbow and seek out a place with his eyes where they could press against each other. If the Earth had caved in under them or the end of the world had come, Vasylyna wouldn't have noticed a thing.

It all passed after she had given birth. It was as if that sweet and foolish itch had never even existed. She would lie down beside her husband, and slowly they would go about their usual perennial business, then turn over back to back – and lay like dead bodies until morning, without even twitching at the break of day.

Vasylyna loved Andriy more than she loved her other sons. She hadn't breastfed any of the others until they were three years old, as she had Andriy. Or else, as she went about her duties in the house, she would suddenly stop and silently stroke the boy's head, or else land a kiss on his ear, so that no one else would see.

If any job was difficult, it would sooner fall to Dmytryk's lot to do it, while Andriy was told to peel potatoes or to go off and pick beet tops for the pigs, so that he would not be exhausted. She wanted her favoured son to retain his male virility and a desire for women, just like his father.

She had pampered him enough. Now Nastunia looked after Andriychyk and molly-coddled him instead of his mother, compensating for the tatty dowry with which she had arrived with caresses and lovemaking. As if there had been no rich farmer's daughter in Tysova

Rivnia for Andriy, he had brought this perforated piece of merchandise all the way from Pidzakharychi. All she had were breasts like those of a wet nurse and a plait dangling down to her ankles.

And now only her breasts, sucked dry by her children, were dangling down. Her plait, cut off at the wedding, lay in a chest in the storehouse. There was no time to play with the plait – she had to be a farmer's wife, even though there was precious little to farm.

Now, however, Andriy would have more property. Dmytryk's share would help.

"ON THE DEER HUNT TOMORROW I'm taking along only Andriy and Mute," Kyrylo told Vasylyna, as he lay out his hunting clothes on the bench in the evening. "Hopefully I won't sleep in."

"And Pavlo? Will he stay behind to peep under Dotsia's skirt? Take him along with you. You'll hunt down more game."

"Foolish woman! You think it will depend on Pavlo, whether we hunt down more game?! Pavlo has work to do. So little of the forest has been chopped down. And now's the time to do it! Winter is knocking at the door. This time last year the felled timber was already drying under an awning, while today the beeches are still growing where the felled timber was meant to be."

"Why do you need Mute? Take Oksentiy instead."

"I told you not to poke your nose into things you don't understand! Mute has a better nose for the game, he's like a dog."

The fellow they called Mute from Tysova Rivnia was born Oleksa Hovdia. He had returned a mute from the

43

Kaiser's war. Shell-shock had taken away his speech, but had also given him a superhuman sense of smell. Mute could smell a fire coming well before the first wisps of smoke had appeared on the horizon.

He could smell out an animal as well as a buck could smell out a doe.

Kyrylo loved Mute and took pity on him, which is why he always took him hunting: it gave the solitary poor fellow some income and assistance. Sometimes he would hire him in place of a gendarme to track down a thief in his forest holdings.

However, there were times when Kyrylo was somewhat afraid of Mute. No, not somewhat afraid, but actually felt mortally afraid of him, when the fellow stared blankly ahead with red eyes, like a bull, his nostrils flaring, and snorting like a smithy's bellows. It seemed as if he could demolish anything in his way then.

Kyrylo had to become a rock when Mute was seized with convulsions, and the fellow rolled about on the ground from pain or sudden loss of consciousness, with white froth oozing from his mouth. Some people said it was a black disease which threw Mute on the ground, that the horrors of war were coming out of him, and that the fellow would soon be able to speak again. But others whispered that it was the devil tormenting him, because he was unable to leave his body.

However, Kyrylo knew perfectly well that you had to avoid angering or scaring Mute.

But when Kyrylo took Oleksa hunting with him, both of them were happy: for only there Mute sensed that he had no disability. He never had a seizure in the forest.

...On Friday morning Vasylyna woke before Kyrylo. For some reason she resisted waking him at first, but when she did rouse him – she was amazed herself. For she had not said a word, as she usually did, but only thoughtlessly touched his forehead with her lips.

And for some reason, she accompanied him into the street, a thing she had never done before, seeing him off into the cold autumn morning.

As Kyrylo dissolved into the mist before her eyes, Vasylyna wanted to call out for him to return, as if she had something important to tell him. But she only waved her hand and returned to the still warm house.

...ON SATURDAY BEFORE THE CRACK OF DAWN, even before the roosters had crowed, someone hammered at the window.

And then Vasylyna only listened to her black misfortune.

Andriy – completely distraught – flew into the house and, without so much as a greeting, blurted out: "Mamma, dad's lost."

"What d'you mean, lost?!" Vasylyna sought out her skirt with one hand and held her night shirt closed with the other, as if hiding from a stranger. "Where is he lost?" She shook Andriy by the chest, staring into his eyes.

"Mum, dad's lost in the forest!" Andriy grabbed a mug of water and emptied it in a single breath, as if he had a great thirst. "We all went in different directions and called out one another, then stopped, because Mute was already driving a deer toward the hide. And when the deer fell into the trap, into the hole we had dug, dad was nowhere to be seen. Mute and I searched for him half the day and all night long. I lost my voice screaming, but dad was nowhere to be found."

"But where did you lose him?" Vasylyna asked, hardly able to hear her own voice, unable to fully comprehend what had happened to her Kyrylo.

"In Boznia."

"And where's Mute?"

"Looking for him. I've come to fetch the boys. We'll keep looking for dad."

"Are you telling me the whole truth, Andriy?" She looked her son in the eyes.

"Why wouldn't I, mother?" he asked, once more filling the mug full of water.

...Frozen and exhausted, the brothers kneaded the forest paths and thickets with their feet for the third consecutive day.

On the first day they had sent Mute back to the village, wracked by fever and suffering seizures several times a day, although at first he had refused to go, waving his arms about, uttering delirious hoarse sounds or trying to weep.

However, he was far too agitated for the Cheviuks to understand what he wanted to say.

Andriy finally forced him down on a stump, pressed down on his shoulders with both hands and said angrily, for some reason, with emphasis, almost yelling:

"Go back to the village! We'll look for him ourselves. You're not to blame if dad is lost or caught up in some trap. We'll find him. Go back home!" Pavlo lifted Andriy's hands off Mute's shoulders: "Why are you yelling at him? He can hear very well. Can't you see that he's scared stiff? Off you go, Oleksa," he almost whispered into the fellow's ear. "And stop shaking so much... Remember, I once fell into a trap as well? Go back to the village. But don't scare the people or mum," Pavlo begged him.

…Oksentiy and Andriy walked along shoulder to shoulder. In silence. Lazily. Pavlo was somewhere way ahead of them, calling out. A crow cawed up above. The wind rustled underfoot.

Andriy stopped, grabbed hold of a maple trunk, stroked it, and then said to Oksentiy, after looking him in the eye for a long time:

"We won't find dad for a while yet."

"What d'you mean?!"

"I know."

"How can you know? Why predict such stupid things?"

"Why ask silly questions? I know, and that's all there is to it. Meanwhile, think hard whether dad has perhaps bequeathed too much to Pavlo."

"What can you do…? Anyway, we'll have to go to the village and call the men to help search for him."

"You idiot!" Andriy hissed. "Idiot. Dad is no longer with us. He's passed away. Dead."

"How do you know?"

"I saw it all! Mute shot him accidentally. He was cleaning his rifle in the evening by the fire in the hut and had a fit. He pressed the trigger. Dad was sitting against the wall, getting dinner ready…

"At first we both ran away. Then in the morning I returned. Obviously, father must have only been wounded at first and tried to save himself. Because I found him by the fire in the middle of the hut. Burnt all over."

"Where was this?"

47

"In Bochkiv."

"So why are we looking for him in Boznia, when we should be in Bochkiv?!"

"Use your brain, you idiot… Use your brain instead of your feet."

…*MARYNKA-GODSPIRIT* appeared at the gate of the Cheviuks' yard on Holy Thursday, while Vasylyna was kneading dough for the Easter breads.

Mrs Cheviuk at first struggled to subdue the malice welling up inside her: it was considered a bad omen to open the door to a visitor while dough was being kneaded for an Easter bread.

But a second later Vasylyna was overcome with a hot flush of guilt: they had said in the village that Marynka-Godspirit had disappeared on Palm Sunday after church service. There had been no one in Tysova Rivnia to worry even for a day what had happened to her, for she was not like Kyrylo Cheviuk: there was no one to pine after her or to go and look for her.

But then Vasylyna became filled with joy as she recalled that Marynka had never visited the Cheviuks with bad news, only to feel everything die inside her: not even Marynka could bring good news to the Cheviuk household now.

Vasylyna dashed out onto the porch, leaving behind her a trail of flour and the spicy smell of vanilla.

"Don't weep, Vasylyna. Kyrylo has been found. But he is not alive," Marynka blurted out in a single breath, settling down on the bench against the house wall. "Tell your sons to go to Bochkiv. To the hut on Ivantsio's Field to remove their father's bones, to bury them before Easter."

"Why Bochkiv? Kyrylo disappeared in Boznia!" Vasylyna almost took a swipe at her.

Marynka got to her feet, came up to Vasylyna wordlessly and stroked her tear-stained face with compassion, then brushed the flour from Vasylyna's skirt and picked off the dough on her fingers.

And then she said:

"I'm telling you, go to Bochkiv! The wolves have eaten him. There are only bones left. I recognized him by his leather belt, which hung on a beam. And your *garchyk* of sauerkraut with the carved deer handle.

I had a dream, Vasylyna. And I heard a voice. The voice said I would find him just before Easter."

Marynka inhaled deeply and exhaled just as deeply. And then she dumbfounded Vasylyna:

"Kyrylo and I were lovers, Vasylyna, back when I was a girl and he a young swain. In that same hut. On Ivantsio's Field. And when he married you for your lands and forests, I wanted to kill myself... And then I wanted to die a second time, when your Dmytryk... but let things be... God is all-seeing. He knows everything...

The Lord gave me back my soul from the other world twice. For this reason I was angry at the Lord. But now I know why He refused to accept my soul: so that I could find my Kyrylo before Easter. In the same spot, where I left him.

Don't be angry with me, Vasylyna... I never did you any harm. My heart betrayed me.

Kyrylo did not die a natural death. I know. There was a hole in his skull.

But he wasn't the kind of man, who would have said farewell to this world and your children, Vasylyna, of his own volition. Not that kind of man... I know."

49

"*...TOMORROW WE'LL START PLOUGHING IN THE MEADOWS,*" Pavlo said over dinner. "Mum will come to bless us."

Dotsia said nothing.

"When you start working the land for the first time after winter, you need to obtain a blessing," Pavlo explained to her for some reason, as if Dotsia was not aware of this. "And we'll be going to our field in The Meadows for the first time."

"May the Lord help us," his wife crossed herself and then unexpectedly stroked her husband's head.

Poor Pavlo. The things they had suffered in the last six months...

They were shadows of their former selves because of father. After everyone had stopped looking, Pavlo kept roaming the forests of Boznia, neglecting his work and his home, as if he was keen on finding treasure there. Then he scoured all the surrounding forests. But he had ventured nowhere near Bochkiv. For Bochkiv was completely in the opposite direction to Boznia. There were six settlements between Boznia and Bochkiv.

And when, after all this, Pavlo had collected his father's bones into a coffin, even a rock would have burst into tears.

Now he had to take care of his mother. She had completely lost her mind after her husband's death. At times she didn't even recognize her own children and grandchildren, or forgot her own name.

She only remembered the festive days and her youthful years.

And each day she asked after her husband:

"Take a look, Dotska, whether my Kyrylo has returned from Shepit yet? He's taking his time, for some reason. Hopefully he hasn't met with any misfortune. People say that wolves have appeared along the river. What do you think, will he be here soon?"

Dotska would wipe away her tears and for the tenth time that day reply:

"Don't worry. He'll be here soon..."

"To hell with misfortune! He's never been so disobedient!"

Fate had obviously meant for Dotska to be a nurse. The two other daughters-in-law didn't even show their faces in their mother-in-law's place. They only looked after their children and pouted their lips, upset that Pavlo had received more of father's holdings than the others. And they took a dislike to Dotsia, for some reason.

And why? Dotsia never even thought ill of them, let so much as said anything against Yelena or Nastunia. Being daughters-in-law is no easy feat...

Pavlo interrupted Dotsia's thoughts with a sigh:

"I never thought such things would happen so soon... Now we have to rack our brains how to manage all the land we've got. Five *falchi* of field is a fair piece of land, after all."

"The Lord will help us," Dotsia stroked Pavlo's head again and pressed up against him with her sunken breasts.

...A pair of well-fed black oxen moved across the boundary of Pavlo's field, formerly Kyrylo's, in The Meadows, when suddenly from the opposite end of the boundary there appeared another pair of oxen, followed by Oksentiy.

"How'd you sleep, brother?" Pavlo called out in greeting and burst out laughing: "Come to help me?"

"I slept on my hand, not my fist. And how about you?" Oksentiy exclaimed merrily and lightly struck the oxen under their tails. "Decided to give your brother a hand?"

The two pairs of oxen stood facing each other, as if ready to do battle.

They breathed heavily, like people with lung disease.

The two brothers breathed heavily as well, standing opposite each other. As if they had just finished ploughing.

Vasylyna was approaching her sons from the stile with a large icon of the Virgin Mary in one hand and a walking stick in the other, followed by Dotsia carrying a basket of food.

"Come to help me plough the field?" Oksentiy asked Pavlo a second time, a grin across his face.

"It's you who probably wants to help me..." Pavlo began uncertainly.

"You think I'm stupid? Not enough of my own land to plough? I just don't understand why you've come onto my land with your oxen?!" Oksentiy continued, the tone of his voice rising. "Have you gone mad, brother, or drunk some poppy-seed milk? This field belongs to me!"

"How's that?"

"Just like that. I have a document to prove it."

"It's me that has a document, not you." From inside his shirt Oksentiy pulled out a rolled-up sheet of canvas tied with red thread and raised it almost to Pavlo's eyes.

...THE VILLAGE ELDER LOOKED FOR A LONG TIME, first at Pavlo, then at Oksentiy. Then he remained silent for a long time. Then he asked the clerk, Johann, for the umpteenth time:

"Johann! Tell me what it says there. Look at Pavlo's document and tell me."

Johann, a small man, who was bent almost double because of a disease in his backbone, strained to look up into the village elder's eyes.

"It says there: 'Upon my death five *falchi* of field in The Meadows and two *falchi* of pasture in The Hollow pass to my son Pavlo Cheviuk'," Johann read slowly, almost letter by letter.

He scanned the document once more in silence.

Then he again looked at the village elder, then at Pavlo and afterwards – at Oksentiy.

"Look at Oksentiy's document and tell us what it says there. But take a good look at the damned thing. Maybe something's fallen into your eye?"

"It says here: 'Upon my death five *falchi* of field in The Meadows and two *falchi* of pasture in The Hollow pass to my son Oksentiy Cheviuk'."

"Either I'm stupid or we all are. The devil should have taken him before birth!" the village elder struck his fist on the desk. "All the same, it seems to me that Kyrylo made out the document for Pavlo... He himself once told me outside the church... My oath, he mentioned leaving things to Pavlo, because he wanted to live out his life with him," the village elder seemed to be talking to himself. "Can you read well?" he asked Johann directly.

"I'm literate," the village clerk retorted, attempting to straighten his broken back as much as he could, but with no success, and he winced with pain, as if he had swallowed a sour crab-apple. "I was tested for writing in Vyzhnytsia. I'm very literate."

"So how can this be?" the village elder asked again, without looking at anyone.

"Dad rewrote his will," Oksentiy answered evenly, keeping his eyes peeled to his document.

It appeared that any moment now he was ready to grab it from the village elder.

But the man sat motionless, the finger of his right hand pressing against Pavlo's document, and the finger of his left hand on Oksentiy's document.

Which is why Johann had to crane his neck even more to read the written text.

"When?!" the village elder and Pavlo asked nervously in unison. And together they turned to face Oksentiy.

"During his lifetime."

"How could he have rewritten it, when he gave each of us a copy in his home and never went to Vyzhnytsia again?!" Pavlo looked at Oksentiy without spite, only in despair. "Did he rewrite it in Bochkiv?! Dad would have told me, if he had changed his mind."

"Johann!" the village elder yelled out, as if the clerk was deaf. "Read it again! Tell us which notary wrote it?"

"Pavlo's document was written by Ursulescu."

"And Oksentiy's?"

"Holstein."

"When was this?"

"Pavlo's – the day after the second Feast of the Blessed Virgin Mary. On the twenty-third of September. Oksentiy's..." Johann began to count, pressing down one finger after another: "Oksentiy's – a day before the Feast of the Presentation of Christ in the Temple. On the third of December."

"What the hell are you saying, Johann?!" Pavlo spat at the ground. "Dad disappeared two days after St Michael's!"

"I don't know…" the clerk shrugged his shoulders. "Two days after St Michael's…" Johann once more silently began to count the days – two days after St Michael's made it the twenty-third of November. But the Presentation of Christ was after the second Feast of the Blessed Virgin Mary. Johann tried to shrug his shoulders. "I don't know how a dead man can rewrite his will. But, sir, his cross is there. See. Look at it, Pavlo." Johann turned both documents around on the desk and showed each man in turn the spot where Kyrylo's signature was: a large cross with all four ends bent down and three neat dots around each of them.

The signatures were identical.

They used such crosses on the Easter eggs painted in Tysova Rivnia. Only Kyrylo Cheviuk signed that way in Tysova Rivnia. Both sons knew that. The village elder knew this too.

"You'll have to go to Vyzhnytsia! I can't do anything here," the village elder finally said, scratching the back of his neck.

"Those who need to, can go. I have no need. I've got my document," Oksentiy made for the door.

"What about mamma? She'd know…" Pavlo said, turning white as parchment, and looking at the village elder.

"Pavlo, you're a smart man. What can you get out of your mother if she forgets her own name on some days?" the village elder dissuaded him. "Your mother won't help you at all. I'm telling you, go to Vyzhnytsia. To the notary."

"Which one?" was all Pavlo could utter. "The first one or the second...?"

"Both of them," sighed the village elder.

...TODOR URSULESCU, a tall thin man in a well-pressed black suit, a white shirt and a bow tie topped by a thin neck, wiped the glass of his pince-nez for the third time and finally perched it upon his nose, tossing the silver chain behind his right ear.

Now the notary looked at Pavlo, who was all hunched up, more affably than before. And he spoke less nervously.

"Yes, of course, Mister Cheviuk..." Ursulescu again glanced at the paper lying before him. "Cheviuk Pavlo. Yes, this document was witnessed by me. On the twenty-third of September. In the presence of your father, Mister Kyrylo Cheviuk, and two witnesses. The document was registered by the senior notary in our office, Doctor Vasylaki. Your father made no alterations or additions to the document. But it is quite likely that he made them on the third of December with the director of our office, Doctor Holstein. Why not with me? Elementary. On the third of December I was in Bucharest at a conference of notaries. And so I couldn't be present."

"But our father disappeared two days before the Feast of St Michael!" Pavlo stood practically on the threshold and forcefully rubbed his palms together, as if it was fiercely cold, even though beyond the open window bees were buzzing and there was a sharp smell of false acacia blossom.

"I don't know, Mr Cheviuk. You'll have to speak to Doctor Holstein. He's a cordial man," Ursulescu smiled with the corners of his lips. But it seemed to Pavlo that his smile was somewhat crafty. "Perhaps you have confused things somewhat? When a client changes the previous provisions of his will, he does so in the presence of witnesses. Their names are registered in our book. A witness can be any legally competent individual. Including public servants, who can bear witness to the identity of a client, if they were previously acquainted with him. Even Doctor Vasylaki could have been a witness. After all, on several occasions previously he had registered sales contracts for parcels of land and forest for your father.

I am ready to believe that your father may have changed his will. But you have not brought the new document, rewritten by your father."

"My brother won't let me have it. And he refuses to come to Vyzhnytsia. And the village elder says that legally my brother is in the right."

"I'll presently let Doctor Holstein know of your delicate matter."

And Todor Ursulescu disappeared with a small file of papers behind a wide door at the end of a long narrow corridor, having first shown Pavlo out of his office.

DOCTOR DAVID HOLSTEIN was seated in a massive wooden armchair with a carved bentwood back in the middle of a large bright office. His feet were set wide apart, his hands clasped firmly around his knees, so much so that two buttons in the middle of his shirt had become undone. The opening in the shirt revealed a thick black tuft of hair on his chest.

Holstein looked like a falcon about to seize its prey.

Pavlo silently squeezed into the office near the door, his green felt hat pressed under his right armpit and the will clasped in his left hand, and shifted his feet.

57

He still hadn't greeted the fellow, when a sudden change came over David Holstein and he frightened poor Pavlo out of his wits.

Holstein jumped to his feet, pushed his shirt into his pants, doing up the buttons as he went, and marched toward Pavlo in broad steps, spreading his arms wide, as if he intended to embrace his visitor. The notary's bloated, freshly-shaven face shone with the sincerest of a good will.

"Mister Cheviuk! Mister Cheviuk! Have you decided to rewrite your will once more?!" the doctor lightly slapped Pavlo on the back. "Good oh. Right! We'll get down to it right away. It won't cost you very much."

Astonished, Pavlo took a step back. But, changing his mind, moved toward the notary.

"I'm not Cheviuk."

Holstein raised his bushy eyebrows very high, as if in surprise, and slapped his hands together:

"What do you mean, you're not Cheviuk?"

"I'm his eldest son."

"Mi-i-ister... That can't be! Such a similarity! Are you unhappy about something? Perhaps you are unhappy about receiving such a large inheritance?"

"Me?!" Pavlo looked about the room for some reason. However apart from them two, there was no one else present. "I received an inheritance? No, I lost it! And I want to know how such a thing could have happened!" Pavlo began to shout.

Now it was Dr. Holstein's turn to take a step back.

"What are you talking about, sir?! And why so emotional?" The notary hurried to his desk, opened a very thick folder and quickly, as if just waiting for the opportunity, poked his fat finger at some piece of paper. "What are you talking about, Mister Cheviuk..." Here's the entry dated December the third last year. The entry says that your father, Kyrylo Cheviuk, son of Ananiy, upon his death leaves his son, Cheviuk Oksentiy, son of Kyrylo, five *falchi* of field in The Meadows and two *falchi* of pasture in The Hollow, thereby annulling the previous will in favour of Cheviuk Pavlo, son of Kyrylo, made on 23 September of the same year. Here, take a look. The signature is your father's."

"But our father disappeared two days after the Feast of St Michael! And St Michael's is always in November. I'm sick and tired of telling everyone this! And you're telling me that father came to you in Vyzhnytsia before the Feast of Christ's Presentation in the Temple! So did he come here after his death then?! Did he change his will when he was a dead man?"

David Holstein must have been a very steadfast man or not easily frightened. He let Pavlo speak his fill, let him become confused about the days, dates and details several times, let him mention a mass of people's names, places and unrelated events. And then his face, crimson from too much emotion, regained its former composure.

Dr. Holstein slowly sat down at his desk, having first just as slowly put on his somewhat tight vest with its silken back.

He rearranged the papers on his desk even more slowly.

Once more he poked his finger at some document known only to him and said softly, but with emphasis, looking Pavlo intently in the eye:

"Esteemed Mister Cheviuk... junior! Please don't forget that you find yourself in a high government institution. Insulting a state public servant while he is in the performance of his duty is punishable under Romanian law. With a fine. A large one. In *lei*[8]. Do you have too many extra *lei* saved up? Where did you get them? Not paying your taxes on time?"

Holstein rose to his feet, rested both his hands on the desk and leaned over toward Pavlo:

"Perhaps when you were the Kaiser's subject that law did not demand punishment for insulting a servant of the state. I don't know. I've forgotten, to be more exact. But now... Now, when there is no one more lawabiding than His Highness the King of Greater Romania... Now, Mister Cheviuk junior, it is obligatorily to adhere to laws. And they apply to you as well, if you'll excuse me. Otherwise I'll be forced to resort to calling the police for help."

"How have I insulted you, mister notary?!" Pavlo spread his arms apart in bewilderment, his felt hat dropping to the floor from under his right armpit. It remained on the floor beside his upturned *postoly* made of thick pigskin. "I merely said that my father disappeared two days after St Michael's. And you're telling me he amended his will before the Feast of Christ's Presentation in the Temple. Where's the insult? The whole of Tysova Rivnia can attest to the fact of the matter. It's the honest truth! May I not live till tomorrow, if I am lying!"

"And when did your father die, mister Cheviuk?"

"Two days after St Michael's."

"Who told you that? Who can testify to this? The fact that your father left home on the twenty-third of November may indeed be the truth. I honestly believe you." Holstein now circled Pavlo, and Pavlo either turned around with his whole body to face him, or merely twisted his

---

8   Romanian monetary unit.

head about. "But who can testify when the actual death took place? Who?"

Pavlo scratched his head.

"Ye-e-es," the notary did not miss a chance to drag out the word. "Yes. You found his purported remains…"

"They weren't remains!" Pavlo again raised his voice. "It was our father. The police attested to it. Half of Tysova Rivnia were witness to it. He had a bump on his head. He was recognized by the bump. And his right knee had once been broken. You could see it on the bones."

"I'm not denying that," the notary said almost gently. "I'm not denying that, mister Cheviuk. But who can attest to the exact date of death of your father? Who? You found his remains on Holy Thursday. Correct?"

"Yes."

"But where was he from the twenty-third of November until Easter? Hah?" the notary looked into Pavlo's eyes. "Perhaps he was hiding for some reason? And who told you that he couldn't have come here on the third of December to amend his will? And then went off and really disappeared?

"You see, mister Cheviuk, the law does not require a client to name the reason he is changing his will. A client has the right to do this. And your father turned up here. He rewrote his will. And went on his way. Incidentally, he was here with a witness. It's written down here. Here we are – Maria Petrusiak, daughter of Ivan, resident of the settlement of Tysova Rivnia, who gave witness as to the identity of your father. Go and ask the witness. And here is the signature of your father on my document. That's his signature. Right?"

Pavlo stood rooted to the ground. He no longer seemed to be listening to the notary.

"...Maria died on Christmas Day," he said softly. "And how could old Mrs. Petrusiak have given witness when she was exactly a hundred years old and blind?!"

"Old age is no impediment to bearing witness, dear mister Cheviuk. As for her neighbour, as she said back then, she could have borne witness as to his identity even in the other world."

"That's a lie, sir!" Pavlo's eyes filled with anger. "All this is a heinous lie! But I don't know how to prove it..." And with all his might he slammed the door shut behind him.

Pavlo stood glued to the door frame of Holstein's office for several minutes, waiting for the notary to dash off to report him to the police.

Meanwhile Dr. David Holstein very calmly opened his safe, placed the folder of documents inside it and poured himself a shot glass of homemade cornel brandy.

The doctor, as he himself realized full well, no longer suffered pangs of conscience.

Two young rams received in remuneration from Cheviuk's fortunate son were not too fatty. They made quite a merry roast.

The money earned in this business by David's resourceful mind now lay in the bank.

Maybe two or three times at the start of this delicate matter the farmer Kyrylo had appeared before him in his dreams. Even now doctor Holstein shrugged his shoulders, remembering the not so pleasant memory: yes... forging a signature was no big deal... But Kyrylo's speech really could not be imitated. He had a unique way of speaking. A colourful language. But these goyim couldn't sense the modulations of their own native language! Its nuances of timbre... Although one couldn't append these nuances to any document.

The cornel brandy was somewhat harsh, but the doctor failed to notice this, and poured himself a second shot glass. What the hell! He could have a third. He wasn't at someone's wake, where you needed to stop at two drinks. And the day had turned out well – thanks to his quick head and clear mind the doctor had looked after himself.

"Long live the king?" he winked at the king's portrait on the wall.

...DOTSKA, WRAPPED IN A BLACK KERCHIEF up to her eyes, tended the Cheviuks' graves.

At first she raked up the dry leaves and pulled out last year's weeds on the graves of her in-laws. Then she hoed the settled earth, trying to avoid the young shoots of the peonies, which were already struggling toward the sun, after which she cleaned up Nastunia's fresh grave from the sides.

She raked up the burnt candle ends and placed them in a clay pot at the head of the grave, and sat a while on the bench at Nastunia's feet.

And prayed.

Crossed herself.

Then set about her work again.

She planted periwinkle on Dmytryk's grave. She still had to loosen the clay a little, to hoe around the lovage, and then it would be time to head back home. Dmytryk asked that she not visit his grave in the cemetery, so as not to tear her heart apart with weeping. Except for perhaps on Christmas Eve and *hrobky*[9]. But he had asked her to plant only periwinkle and lovage on his grave. The

---

9   Literally, "graves". On the Sunday after Easter people visit the graves of their relatives and bring along Easter cake, Easter eggs and food and drink to offer to others to remember their relatives.

periwinkle would stay green all year long and the lovage would be fragrant.

Dotska would have planted periwinkle on his grave anyway. For the lad had never worn a periwinkle garland on his head in this world[10], so at least it could flower blue for him in the other world. The lovage was not waiting for the sun to appear either and was rushing to break free of the earth, sending its fragrance in all directions, as soon as one brushed against its leaves. Let it smell. Maybe that smell would somehow reach Dmytryk's soul in the other world.

Dotsia didn't even wipe away the salty tears that fell from her eyes. At least she could cry as much as she wanted here and wordlessly talk her fill. Most of all – with her father-in-law and Dmytryk.

Even though her father-in-law was a very hard man, he never let anyone wrong his daughtersin-law. Not even the most frivolous one among them…

Why bandy words about? While people sit in judgment – there is no justice. The Lord will judge everyone according to their conscience and the truth.

And he would judge Yelena with her own truth and her easy ways.

And Oksentiy with Andriy as well.

Only Dmytryk would not be judged. But even if he had been judged, it would have made no difference to Dmytryk. He was buried in the clay because of his young blood.

And what about Petrunia? She farmed as she grew old and grew old as she farmed.

And who was it all for?

---

10   That is, he had never been married. During the marriage ceremony the bride and groom each wore a garland of periwinkle on their head.

The Lord had given them no children.

And they had nothing good, apart from their farm.

Ivan beat Petrunia almost black and blue nearly every week.

He didn't let her venture into the village on her own.

At parties he stayed at her side and stopped her from dancing with strangers.

Everyone knew this now. So they stopped inviting her to dance, even at weddings, so as to avoid Varvarchuk's anger.

Perhaps the only good times the woman had ever known were with Dmytryk... Lord, forgive Dotsia such foolish sinful thoughts. And where had such a thing entered her head? In the cemetery...

The lovage had come up very thick this year. She would just loosen the earth a little around it and set off home, because her heart could explode from grief here. In a month they would be celebrating *hrobky* in the village. Everything had to look good and proper around the grave...

Oh, good and proper ...

In Tysova Rivnia people were already saying: '*Any which way, but not like the Cheviuks.*'

What could she say...

It had all passed. Everything.

Her ever-spiteful mother-in-law was long dead.

The three brothers now avoided each other even from afar and had not spoken with one another for God knows how long, even outside church at Easter. And yet they all stood in the same spot in church. Grandpa Ananiy, Kyrylo's father, had stood there. They stood shoulder to shoulder. Easter basket to

65

Easter basket. They drank and chatted with strangers. But said not a word to each other. They parted, heading for their homes from church without giving each other so much as an Easter egg, or an Easter cake in memory of the souls of their father and mother.

How could the parents' souls look at all this from the other world?! All this could make one die a second time.

Even the priest had tried to make peace among the brothers.

But no way, Your will be done, Lord!

Andriy became a widower.

Pavlo lost his health.

Only Oksentiy was like a stallion. Unable to feed his backside hay[11], just like his Yelena.

Their life with Pavlo progressed slowly without the land in The Meadows. They saved for a long time and finally had enough to buy three *falchi* of good field from Kulierka near The Mills. It would be enough to last them and their children. If only there would be no war. Or some other misfortune...

"May the Lord help you, Odokiyka!" a familiar male voice frightened Dotsia. Its owner had obviously been standing behind her for some time.

Dotsia got to her feet and wiped her eyes.

"Is that you, Hrytsko? What are you doing here?" she asked Keyvan, her closest neighbour.

In the autumn he had fallen from the Jew's mill and had become feeble-minded, which was why he went about with his head wrapped in a woman's woolen shawl, over which he wore a felt hat with the brim flattened out.

---

11 A Hutsul dialectical expression meaning "unable to calm down, to be at ease, to restrain one's desires and capricious whims".

"I'm thinking."

Dotsia looked at her neighbour and shrugged her shoulders.

"You've nothing left to think about. Leave the thinking for later."

Keyvan sat down on the bench beside the stone crypt of the local priests, the Volianskys, located next to the graves of the Cheviuks, and looked at Dotsia with strange eyes.

"People always have things to think about, Odoki-yka… As you can see, I've grown old, but my sins will not age with me. They won't let me sleep. Or die…" her neighbour looked at her strangely and spoke in a strange manner.

Without straightening up, Dotsia handed him a jug of water. He was weak. Perhaps he could sense his death approaching. And he needed to talk.

"Who can sleep peacefully with their sins?" she asked and answered her own question: "No one."

"Listen, woman, I've come to tell you something," Hrytsko rose with unexpected haste from the bench and painfully grabbed hold of her elbow. "I know I can't die until I tell you something."

"I've known for a very long time what you want to tell me, Hrytsko…" Dotsia sharply freed her elbow.

"What do you know?!"

"… About Dmytryk…" Dotsia remained silent for a while. "The devil had confused you back then, making you help send someone into the other world. But the Lord has already punished you. Made you feeble-minded. In the very same spot. Near the mill. So there's no need to tell me anything. I've known for a long time."

She dispatched Hrytsko without a drop of pity, as she stroked the clay on Dmytryk's grave.

Keyvan remained silent for a long time, as if he wasn't surprised by what he had heard.

"That's not what I came to tell you… You can kill me right here and now, but it was me who bore witness in the name of the late Kyrylo." He blurted it out quickly, as if afraid someone would try to stop him.

"Where did you bear witness, Hrytsko?!"

Dotsia held the hoe in her hand the way people held an axe before driving it into a log.

"Where did you bear witness?!"

"In Vyzhnytsia. At the Jewish notary's. Andriy talked me into bearing witness, after his father had disappeared. Andriy made me do it."

Hrytsko stayed silent, as if trying to recall something or choosing his words. And then he said:

"Oksentiy gave Andriy a bull, a pregnant heifer and two or three sheep to find someone who would come along to the notary's to confirm that he was their father. I don't know if they bribed the notary…

Who could Andriy have turned to, but me?

Oksentiy paid me off with a barren cow and two *kopy* of maize stalks. We fetched the horses in the evening. Late at night, so no one would see, we set off for Vyzhnytsia. Oksentiy and Andriy spent the night in Vyzhenka at grandma Khymka's place and I went off to the local smithy. We'd fought together with him during the war.

In the morning each of us set off separately for Vyzhnytsia. In Lazar's inn on the outskirts of the city they dressed me in your father-in-law's sheepskin coat and hat. Remember, your late father-in-law wore a white sheepskin coat with a black collar? And a hat made of hare. They tied a shawl around the right side of my face, as if a pustule had appeared there. We arrived at the notary's office. I confirmed that I was Kyrylo Cheviuk. I said that I had changed my mind and wanted to rewrite my will to favour Oksentiy, rather than Pavlo. And then I signed with exactly the same cross your father used. I bent each end down. And placed a dot on three of the ends. Exactly the way Kyrylo did it. Back in the Kaiser's army I had learned to forge signatures. Andriy had shown me his father's cross under his will."

Hrytsko twirled the felt hat about in his hands. Without the hat his elongated head, wrapped in a shawl with large roses in the middle, looked like a pumpkin.

But Dotska failed to notice this. She seemed to have turned to stone from genuine horror and pain, still grasping the hoe.

"I couldn't refuse Andriy, Dotska...

I could have refused Varvarchuk, when he told me that Dmytryk had to be done in because of Petrunia... But I didn't. Because I had returned from the war. I had my own spleen to vent then. Near my heart. On the left side. And Varvarchuk had his own."

Hrytsko continued to fidget with his hat. For a moment Dotska thought that at some other time she would have warned her neighbour to stop doing that. His head was tormenting him enough as it was. He kept turning his hat about, which would make it hurt even more.

Dotska did not listen to her inner voice for long, because Hrytsko talked without taking his eyes off her, and this made her flesh creep.

"And much later, after Dmytryk had passed away, when my mother had become blind and I needed to feed my gaggle of children, I could no longer refuse Andriy.

Because he could have told people that it was me and Ivan who had worked over your Dmytryk... And I felt so bad then, so bad.

May the Lord punish me for all the bad I've done in this world. Because the people won't have a chance to do so..."

"Why did you drag your blind mother into all this?" Dotska asked almost indifferently.

"That wasn't mother. Mother was closer to God
at the time than to mortal life. It was my wife dressed as
my mother. She could play blind... And I made
her do it, because I had reason to. May the two of them
rest here with the Lord..."

PART TWO

FARE YE WELL, FATHER

"THE APPROACHING WINTER WILL BE WARM. See, how thin the pig's spleen is?" noted Mykhailo Strynada, shaking the steaming entrails before the farmer's eyes. "May we be healthy as ever, but something will soon happen in this world. A warm winter never bodes well."

"Whatever the Lord gives, is ours to bear," Havrylo Diachuk replied indifferently to the pig slaughterer, bringing in the wooden troughs for the fresh meat and placing them on either side of the butcher. "You can place the meats in this trough, the bacon in this one, and you can put the head, trotters and skin for the jellied meats in this one."

In reply Strynada only smiled wordlessly into his bushy moustache, which was turned magnificently upwards, and continued to work on the carcass, which had been split in two.

In Tysova Rivnia he was nicknamed Potash. As soon as anyone in the village became ill or fell into despair, Strynada, who was as talkative as an old granny, would offer the inevitable piece of advice:

"Slake some potash and give him some to drink – he'll feel better straight away. I cure myself from all kinds of pain and illness this way."

And so the farmers who vied for the butcher's services in the days before the winter festivals of St Nicholas, Christmas, Easter or even before such great celebrations as weddings or christenings, kept handy for Strynada some soda, which people called "potash" in these mountains. If you didn't keep the butcher happy, the freshly-slaughtered meat would not be as tasty.

He was truly a master of his trade, famous well beyond Tysova Rivnia.

The Jewish merchants from Vyzhnytsia sent not just simple one-horse carts, but entire fiacres[12], which in the summer were lined with ice, to collect the black pudding, liverwurst and home-style sausages made by Strynada,. Everything of his hand was so tasty you could gnaw your fingertips off. And that not to mention the oven-baked salceson[13], the *spovyvantsi*[14] smothered in snow-white lard, the hams smoked with fragrant plum-tree logs. The highlight of his craft was the fatback bacon[15], cured in brine and aromatic plant oils and then rubbed with garlic and cayenne.

Lavish fiacres, usually assigned to take wealthy noblemen on outings, harnessed to two spirited horses, were crammed full in Tysova Rivnia with every kind of sausage and salceson, and then driven like crazy to restaurants in Chernivtsi; and the hams, as pink as blushing brides, and the salted meats, which could be eaten with lips alone, once again surrounded on all sides with nettle greens and blocks of ice, left at breakneck speed from Chernivtsi in the freight cars of express trains bound for Viennese shops and markets, theatre buffets, and the homes of especially wealthy citizens in the vast Danube monarchy.

---

12   Fancily decked-out horse-drawn covered vehicles with doors, usually reserved for transporting the rich.

13   Salceson (*saltseson*) is a type of sausage found in Western Ukrainian and Polish cuisine, similar to presswurst. Usually made by filling a pig's stomach with coarsely diced meat, internal organs and fat. This is then baked or boiled, and smoked. There are several varieties of salceson, which depend on the ingredients: black 'salceson' contains blood, white 'salceson' is made with a mixture of seasoned meats without blood and *ozorkowy* (tongue) 'salceson' is mainly composed of pork or veal tongue.

14   *Spovyvantsi* – a meat dish. Slices of raw meat are filled with pork fat and rolled up, then tightly tied with string and smoked over a fire or fried in lard.

15   Fatback bacon is widely eaten throughout Europe. In Italy it is called *lardo*, in Ukraine – *salo*.

However, on this day Havrylo Diachuk did not dwell on the virtues of the village butcher. He had other things on his mind. His heart was being torn apart now, just like that small intestine in Strynada's hands scalded by hot pig swill, which the butcher had just tossed into the waste bucket.

Any other time such an occasion as awaited the Diachuk household in the coming days would have resulted in a father's heart beating in his chest like a wild *hutsulka* dance or a lively highland *kosa*[16], instead of ticking hollowly, as if after silent weeping.

Was it not a reason to be overjoyed, that your only orphaned daughter, who was raised without a mother's love and knowledge, was being taken for a wife by such a dignified farmer? And that the butcher, who supplied small goods to the table of the Kaiser himself, would be cooking the wedding deer and hare dishes for the simple Diachuks, who hailed from the most outlying settlement in Tysova Rivnia?

But today Havrylo's heart was not beating to the rhythm of a *hutsulka* or *kosa*. His heart drew in like a snail or a hedgehog, as if out of fear, and then pounded like mad against his ribs. He was already extremely furious with himself and with all the servants. He had just bawled out the maid, which he had never done before.

A jug of cream had slipped out of his weakened hands.

He had whipped his cow under the tail for no reason at all.

He had tossed a billet of wood at the vociferous rooster, almost breaking its legs.

What was all this about?

---

16 *Kosa* – a slow wedding dance with special movements.

Well, maybe it was because the groom was twice the age of the bride? That was true.

Well, if it came to that, the groom was even older than his future father-in-law. His tomorrow's son-in-law was in fact older than Havrylo.

But was this uncommon in their mountains?

Other mothers would have willingly laid themselves down under such a son-in-law, if only he would have taken their daughter into his household.

Havrylo's future son-in-law had so much land and livestock, that any criticism of him was probably no more than licentious gossip on old women's tongues.

Although he was somewhat quirky, *z fukom*, as the locals said.

But what about Havrylo himself? Was he beyond reproach when he thrashed his innocent wife, just because that's what all the other men in the mountains did?!

His arms should have withered back then!

It was true. Every man had his quirks. However, an annoying thought was gnawing at his parental heart. And Havrylo felt that he was preparing for a wake, rather than a wedding.

There in the doorway of the barn stood his little pussycat, his little *mytska*, his only child.

As white as the mist hanging over their settlement after the rains.

Innocent as the apple blossom in May.

Looking at her father with eyes that were not joyous, but neither were they sad – and she seemed to want to tell him something.

Perhaps she wished to ask him how he intended to live among these hills without her?

Or perhaps to ask him, why he was marrying her off to a man whom she had seen for the first time during the matchmaking ceremony, and had immediately fainted when she learnt why he had entered their house.

Or did she want to nestle up to her father's chest, so that he could console this child of his, who had not yet fully comprehended that in a few days she was to become a married woman.

Or perhaps she wanted to know how she would start her new life tomorrow, although not in a strange land, but nevertheless away from home?

The sudden unexpected emotion which swept over him brought tears to Havrylo's eyes. He grabbed the axe and went off into the woodshed. For a long time he rearranged the already neatly-stacked firewood, split several logs into splinters for no reason at all, then kicked these about the shed and settled down on the bench against the wall. But not for long.

Havrylo smoked his pipe only a few times a year: at the start and end of both Christmas and Easter Lents. At the start of Petrivka[17] too. And on the anniversary of his wife's sudden death.

But this time he fidgeted for a long while under the beam, until he found the hidden tobacco leaves wrapped in paper and a piece of cowhide.

The excessively dry, but still fragrant tobacco leaf crackled compliantly between his fingers, but it was difficult to pack into the pipe – and the lazy, but aromatic smoke was already weaving its way through cracks in the woodshed.

Meanwhile Havrylo unblinkingly stared at the inclined head of his child and only sighed. Her tender figure remained motionless in the doorway to the barn.

---

17 Petrivka – a fasting period beginning in the second week after Trinity Sunday and ending on the Feast of Saints Peter and Paul (12 July).

Departed granny Kalyna, his maternal grand-mother, had once told Havrylo a peculiar story. An underage fool, she had heard that her father was marrying her off to the village bailiff, who was a widower with three children. Excited, she had chased about the house with joyous shouts, like a calf released to pasture after a winter in the shed, jumping about and yelling: 'I'm getting married! At last I'm getting married! Lordy-Lord, I can't wait for tomorrow to come!'

His child hadn't said a word to him, neither a kind word, nor a harsh one. It was as if nothing had happened.

Only his *kuma*[18] Paraska had clapped her hands upon hearing who had made a match with her goddaughter:

"You should have promised her to someone who was three moments away from death, Havrylo! She would have been able to marry a second time sooner! As it is, she will only suffer and give rise to fits of jealousy. That will be her only joy in life! Have you got ten daughters, that you're in such a hurry to offload her onto someone else's shoulders?!" Havrylo didn't utter a word in reply.

And he thought: was it indeed his fault that another man had fallen for his daughter and wanted to marry her? He was giving her away to someone who had taken a fancy to her. No one else had approached him.

The girl was already in her fifteenth year. Even cream soured on milk, if it wasn't skimmed off.

Havrylo surveyed his yard – and already it did not appear so sweet and dear to him, as it had the day before.

There was a burning sensation below his chest, similar to heartburn. But he could not extinguish this pain with tobacco or thoughts.

---

18 *Kuma* – form of addressing the godmother of a child; used by parents of the child when referring to their child's godmother.

Meanwhile butcher Strynada had risen to his feet over the steaming troughs and was merrily chatting with the cook.

The bridesmaids were silently cutting coloured foil to make flowers for the wedding tree.

Tomorrow's bride, her hair in wooden rollers, skulked about the yard as if she had been given a hiding, seeking a spot where people would leave her in peace.

Havrylo continued smoking in the woodshed. The burning sensation in his chest became so intense, that he felt as if he was about to turn into a smoked ham.

RED-FACED, HAVRYLO moved among the wedding guests, holding a miniscule shot glass half filled with vodka, at the same time managing to bark orders to the musicians and the cook, and to exchange a word or two with the guests of the groom as they were sitting down at the table to the right of his only joy – the princess of the wedding.

The guests who had come from other districts were especially noisy and merry.

Was it because the bride was so much to their liking, her face framed in a mass of ribbons and small bells?

Or were they glad that Havrylo had not refused holding a joint wedding[19], having just one decent reception, the likes of which the world had never seen?

Perhaps the guests were pleased that two farmers were combining their farms into one?

---

19 According to Hutsul custom the wedding was held in two homes – separately in the home of the bride and the groom. This was a sign of wealth. When the guests of the bride and groom celebrated in one place, it was considered a more modest wedding reception.

Or envious of the young and innocent package coming into the arms of such an old bachelor, who had at last dared to end his tiresome single life?

The young prince – and that was really stretching the meaning of the word - had just "bought" the bride from her father and was now eyeing her with stern eyes. Was he only playing at being formidable and in fact rejoicing at his redolent flower?

He had bought Havrylo's darling with his immense landholdings. He wasn't expecting a dowry with her, but had instead doubled Diachuk's wealth. The young couple would be living in the village, in the home of the groom.

But that was good. Why did his child have to stare at these endless hills for the rest of her life? A village was a village, after all. You could go off to church there. Chat with people. Take some cream to Vyzhnytsia to sell at the market. Buy something from the Jewish merchant. It was more fun than staring into space here waiting for someone to come up from the valley so that you could exchange a few words with them.

Havrylo toasted the groom, bowed in all directions before the guests and once more hurried up to the cook, urging her to bring hot dishes to the tables more often – so they wouldn't go cold...

Today Havrylo was overjoyed. He would have loved to sit down at a table and sing, if it weren't for the fact that he had to bark orders at the women helping out at the wedding and to keep a watch on the cook and musicians, to make sure the guests were satisfied.

Several days before the wedding he had felt like gadflies had bitten him all over.

E-e-eh... something stupid had come into Havrylo's head in a fit of temper then! Women had to put up with older men. Anyway, the older a bull was, the easier it could inseminate a heifer. And Havrylo needed grand-children. So the bride should be happy that she got her-self a business-minded and sedate husband, rather than some chimneysweep. It would be easier to make friends with other farmers while being at this fellow's side.

There you go!

An inexpressible joy puffed out Diachuk's chest, as if he himself was getting married on this day. Small won-der. Havrylo was a dignified man. He valued honour above all else. And what honour today's bride was bring-ing him! The whole world was listening and even more people would know, because Tysova Rivnia was as long as a woman's tongue! He should have invited more guests to the wedding.

He should have! As it was, Havrylo had succumbed to his stupid thoughts and the pitiful eyes of his daughter, and had invited fewer people than he had wanted to in-vite. A child was a child, to be educated and led out into the world. And his heart had softened then because of the pitiful sobs of his only daughter...

As the guests drifted off to sleep, a lone unappeased guest drawled drunkenly in the *shopa*[20] as a result of the generous regaling:

> *Oh, the cuckoo cooed,*
> *And rested on a rock.*
> *This night at midnight,*
> *Will be amen for the c...t*[21]

---

20 A temporary wooden structure of large proportions which could accom-modate 200-300 guests. It was adorned with carpets and paper flowers. Tables were set up in a rectangle on its perimeter, and one table ran down the middle from end to end (author).

21 Obscene, meaning female sexual organ. In the Hutsul dialect the word is *potka*.

The late night echo carried the bawdy wedding song across the sleepy hills and valleys, preparing the boundless surroundings of the settlement, now resting quietly for a few hours, for the next day.

If only this wedding night would hurry and pass!

Havrylo decided to keep watch over the door from the entrance hall to the guest-room, where the bride and groom had gone to bed. He skulked back and forth, in no hurry to go to sleep. Everyone was already asleep. The cook was snoring in the niche behind the oven. And the snoring of the musicians could be heard all the way from the barn. Guests from further afield had already bedded down in the wedding *shopa* on the benches and tables, glad that the hosts hadn't taken all the food away into the cellar.

Havrylo was aware that too much alcohol or simply curiosity could lead some guest to tug at the door latch to the married couple's room. Even though he had raced about all day long and was almost falling off his feet, Havrylo refused to entrust such an important matter as watching over the young couple's first sleepless night to his *kuma* Paraska.

No way in hell!

This was a discrete matter.

It wasn't as simple as removing a bung from a wine barrel...[22]

... Havrylo was moving among the tables of guests a second time.

He had already managed an apt reply to the piquant jokes of the musicians and his *kuma* Paraska.

---

22 A metaphor for the act of defloration. Despite their very obvious straightforwardness about life, the Hutsuls often used metaphorical phrases to describe various physiological acts.

Twice he had sent the cook off to attend to the oven.

He had already managed to berate his neighbour Kateryna, who he thought was washing the crockery far too slowly.

Meanwhile the young couple, sitting in their place under the icons in the centre of the *shopa*, still had not summoned the father for the ancient ritual after the nuptial night.

The groom, with his back to the bride, spent a long time haggling loudly with Makoviy Tomniuk over two *prazhyny*[23] of highland plateau on Magura, so loudly that all the animated guests heard him. As if there was no other place or time to conduct this business.

For a moment Havrylo was even furious. Where had anyone seen such a thing at a Hutsul wedding, where the groom, without having publicly thanked the father for his daughter's virginity, negotiated some business, rather than his honour?! This wasn't Christian!

But Havrylo tried to placate himself with the thought that perhaps it was better that his son-inlaw was delaying with this sweetest of moments for all fathers? Perhaps it was better this way, so that all the wedding guests could see what a successful famer had joined Havrylo's household.

Because everyone could see that even at the wedding table, even after his first night with the bride, he was already thinking about expanding his farm.

He was already thinking about his family's wealth, even in front of all these honest people, assembled here, even at his own wedding reception!

Soon he would be thanking the father, for his right hand was already holding the wooden tumbler, which he

---

23 *Prazhyna* – a measure of land, equal to $1/80^{th}$ of a *falcha* = 163.3 square metres; for comparison, one acre = 4,046.8 square meters.

himself had placed on the table beforehand, as custom demanded.

Beautifully proportioned, ingeniously carved and even more imaginatively encrusted with tiny white beads, the tumbler was about three-quarters of a forefinger high. Made from softwood, it stood in all its splendour before the groom on a tray decorated with equally pure-white beads.

Only at first glance did the tumbler appear to be ordinary.

In actual fact it had a very simple, but at the same time perfectly ingenious secret, and the future of today's bride depended on the disclosure of this secret.

A wooden tumbler such as this, with its secret bottom, told the assembled guests a lot about the bride without any words needing to be stated, without any gratitude being expressed or exclamations uttered. For this tumbler was the modest creation of some eminent woodcarving master – the sole public indicator of a bride's honour or disgrace. Of her chastity and innocence. Of her once-in-a-lifetime triumph and the only lasting superiority of the girl-woman over her husband.

This brief celebration, this momentary superiority in one thing alone: the proof of her virtue beyond a shadow of a doubt. The alternative would be her public disgrace.

The public affirmation by the groom of his bride's intact honour, affirmed not so much her reputation, as much as the honour and pride of her parents.

And these two notions – honour and pride – meant as much as landholdings and wealth to the patriarchal and exceedingly superstitious highlanders.

Oh, yes! The person who had first dreamed up this tumbler, so cunning in its faultlessness, had obviously been a great master of intrigue and fantasy.

Perhaps he had even been a bit of a Jesuit, or perhaps a closet executioner.

Or perhaps a mortally offended egotist...

That eternally long moment preceding the denouement to the most important of the wedding intrigues had cost some people here in the mountains not only their health, but their lives as well.

The tongues of so many people had become broken in these parts, and so many had turned red or swollen over conversations about intact or perforated wedding tumblers!

The torrents of tears that had been shed by mothers, publicly disgraced by their sons-in-law!

The countless number of beech cudgels which had been administered by humiliated fathers upon the backs of mothers for the public shaming of their daughters!

And the number of punches received by daughter-brides from their husbands, upon whom fell half the shame of their young wives!

Meanwhile the secret of the tumbler was quite simple, like everything in this world. The secret was hidden in... its base.

For the ancient Hutsul custom prescribed that on the day after the first wedding night, before all assembled wedding guests, the elder master-of-ceremonies made the honorary toast on behalf of the groom, a toast of gratitude to the father of the bride.

The father of the bride would come up to the table at which the young couple was seated. The groom would take the small tumbler in his right hand, covering the bottom with his forefinger, while at the same time the master-of-ceremonies filled the tumbler to the brim with vodka. With the words: 'I drink to you, father', the groom would upend the tumbler without removing his finger from the bottom, after which he would replace the tumbler on the table, still holding his finger in place, and the elder master-of-ceremonies would again fill the tumbler to the brim..

And at this moment the high point of the ritual would be reached.

Bending across the table, the groom would hand over the full tumbler to the bride's father with the words: 'May you be healthy, father!' and then remove his fingers from the tumbler.

At this moment the wedding *shopa* would resemble a hall in which a deceased person was lying in a coffin.

Suddenly complete silence would fall, so that one could hear fruit compote gurgling in a person's throat or a rooster crowing outside.

The necks of the wedding guests became elongated, like a goose's crop.

The drummer might sometimes thump the taut skin of the drum every so often for the ceremony's atmosphere.

To such an accompaniment of silence and a lazy drum beat the father of the bride would quickly upend the tumbler into his mouth.

And what the first wedding night had been like for the groom, was reflected in the reaction of the tumbler of vodka.

If the bride was intact, the groom would have chosen a tumbler for the toast... with an intact bottom.

But if she had not been intact... then that tumbler's cunning secret would come into play.

According to custom, in the barn next to the intact tumbler, there stood another one, whose bottom had a barely-visible hole drilled into it. Such a miniature hole through which, if need be, the liquid could escape, as an affirmation of the fact that the groom had taken for a wife a girl who had been drilled through by someone before him.

After the first night the groom would go into the barn, fetch both tumblers, and then place the one he needed on the table before him, thus concealing the secret of the honour or shame of his young bride until the last moment.

... AND SO HE STOOD all flustered, eye to eye with his son-in-law, and a pleasant impatience cooled Havrylo Diachuk's joyous chest. Greedily his eyes caught the equally greedy, but languid tension of his son-in-law's Adam's apple, because the fellow drank the vodka, as if he was drinking it for the first time in his life, as if he was relishing May honey[24], instead of fierce plum vodka.

Then the son-in-law sharply lowered the tumbler to the table, still keeping his finger on its bottom and smiled broadly at Havrylo.

The elder master-of-ceremonies very slowly filled the tumbler to the very top, as if he were filtering rather than pouring the drink.

"To your good health, dad!" the hithertotaciturn groom almost yelled out and raised the tumbler almost to Havrylo's mouth, his finger still pressed to the bottom.

Diachuk took hold of the tumbler when it was right next to his lips, and in his joy he encircled it with his

---

24 The first honey of the season was collected in May and was considered the best.

whole hand, but the bottom, released by the groom's hand, unexpectedly exuded a thin relentless stream of vodka, like a sudden summer shower.

Still unable to comprehend the horror of the moment, Havrylo instinctively kept inclining the tumbler toward his mouth, but the glistening stream flowed down his chin and trickled under the collar of his embroidered shirt, obviously in an attempt to reach his very heart.

Deafening sighs, sounding like thunder on a bright sunny day, shook the hushed *shopa*. The 'ahs' of the women intermixed with the 'ohs' of the men became drowned in the loud hubbub of the awakened drum.

But this strange concoction of discordant and disorganized sounds interrupted the bellow of the mortally-wounded buck: Havrylo looked in horror inside the suddenly empty tumbler and tossed it to the ground. With both hands he tore at his shirt,bellowing at the ceiling of the *shopa*: "No!!!"

Suddenly turning black as night, the father of the bride stood crucified upon the two lengths of linen of his torn shirt, his arms thrust wide apart, and a black cloud of invisible shame covered his still young head in a wave of momentarily dimmed intellect.

"No..." Diachuk only rattled away now, but no one heard him above the insane din of the drum. The wedding guests tucked into their food and drink, as if nothing had happened, while the intoxicated married women hacked at Havrylo's heart and openly, publicly ridiculed the farmer, who was torn asunder with shame, intentionally singing heartless bawdy wedding songs at the tops of their voices, for all the hills to hear:

> *On the far side of the torrent*
> *Eggshells float quickly past,*

The wild girls offer lads their c…s
In honour of the dead.

… PETRUNIA BOLTED the house shut from the inside. She tugged at the wooden key several times to make sure that she had locked it properly and then, closing the door to the entrance hall with a dull thud, she walked into the guest room, its windows facing the orchard. No one would disturb her here, nor could they eavesdrop on her. And she couldn't express her thoughts out loud – she couldn't do that: everything was kept under lock and key.

Everything.

Her heart.

And tongue.

And memory.

All the same, this room was not for her.

It was for guests.

For years it stood closed – all the doors, windows and cracks sealed shut, like a virgin before marriage.

She could sense the stale air in here.

Because the woman of the house had failed to shake out the carpets and rugs.

Failed to dry out the kerchiefs and *keptars*.

Had not placed dry basil and tansy between the sheepskin coats.

She was indifferent to everything.

Guests never visited their house.

And she rarely squeezed herself in here.

Except perhaps to have a good cry, so that no one would see her.

And to press her baby to her breast.

This was the only place where she had neither shame, nor pity – she only wept tears here. Harsh tears, like the unripe gooseberries she had once tasted in her father's orchard.

Petrunia buried her face in a mountain of magnificent cushions. She could lie there crying until evening, until those disgusting bulls and cows began to trumpet their presence from the stable, as if blowing into funerary *trembitas*[25] with their hungry muzzles.

Let them die! How their lowing bored into her ears!

Nothing would happen to them.

Hunger was nothing compared to shame. They would survive.

She knew of things far worse than hunger…

… God, how had she lived down the shame and not finished herself off?

By drowning herself in a torrent of water.

Or hanging herself from a fir tree.

Instead she went out among the people.

And asked them: 'How are things?'

Answered their 'good-days'.

… But the people were indifferent to what was in her heart.

God only knew whether they gossiped about her or kept silent.

She didn't ask anyone.

But if the truth be known, they didn't spit on the ground after she passed by.

---

25 A *trembita* or shalm is a long wooden trumpet, up to several meters long, which highlanders used to communicate with one another.

So, cry your fill, little girl, till you choke, but don't expect any pity from anyone. No one will ever take pity on you.

Petrunia shifted the wet hair from her forehead and sat down on the bed, supported on all sides by cushions.

She sat looking exactly like a bride. Hair unbraided. Eyes dulled from tears and despair.She looked at the orchard. And in the orchard everything looked as it had when they sewed her wedding garland; green branches were rocking in the wind and some foolish birds twittered, as they flitted from tree to tree.

She would have flitted like them too, from hill to hill, not only from tree to tree, if only she could avoid hearing that loathsome music which burst through the walls, like a mad dog yelping. The drummer seemed to have completely lost his mind – he was flaying the drum, as if he was bashing her over the head.

And auntie Paraska, her godmother, was brushing her hair and slicing through her with words, as sharp as the knives used by butcher Strynada:

> *Don't cry, don't cry, dear little bride, –*
> *There is no need to cry.*
> *Because you know, that there is no*
> *Village for virgin girls.*
> *There's no village for virgin girls,*
> *Nor one for young fellows.*
> *Don't cry, don't cry, dear little bride,*
> *There is no need to cry.*

Auntie Paraska perhaps had nothing to cry about. But it would have been easier for Petrunia to choke on her tears than to think about old Ivan, who had agreed with her dad to take her hand in marriage. And oh, today the musicians were already playing wedding melodies.

No, she bore her father no ill will. Who could have refused such a rich man?! But, holy Lord in Heaven, how old her groom was! The threshing stick in their barn was younger than her Ivan. After the match was made, Petrunia's father had told her in a hushed voice to address her husband using the polite form of '*vy*'[26].

Didn't she know that herself? How could her tongue have formed the sound of *ty* in her mouth, when Ivan (may wild bears tear him apart!) was older than her father? And her father was still full of life! He could marry again!

While that Ivan... my God, always going about unshaven, looking like the Gypsy tinsmith from the neighbouring village. She feared Ivan more than sudden death.

And he was already dragging her into the house, even though the wedding guests were still drinking and carousing, stuffing their faces, and for some reason he locked the door from the inside. And his hands were trembling, as if he was about to steal something...

...PETRUNIA BRAIDED HER HAIR painstakingly, so that not a single strand would appear from under her kerchief. She wiped her face dry of tears with the hem of her skirt and took the baby out from under the cushions.

Oh, Lordy-Lord... Had her mother known... had her father known... they would probably have beaten her with beech sticks. Mercilessly.

But her mother was rotting in the earth.

---

26   The French use the polite form of address *vous* and the familiar form *tous*; similarly in Ukrainian the polite form is *vy* – reserved for older or respected people, and the familiar form is *ty* – for addressing those of one's own age, close friends and family.

And her father no longer acknowledged her as his child. He had cursed her.

Lordy-Lord, what things had come to…

Were a stranger to see her, he would have said – she's lost her mind.

She would have thought the same herself, had she seen everything as a bystander and not known the truth.

But what did she care what someone else thought? Whatever anyone wanted to think – they had done it long ago and perhaps forgotten all about it.

It was all the same to her. She pressed her baby to her bosom and smelt its fragrant little face, rubbed with mint and chamomile.

Who cared that her child was made of rags.And its head was a yellow reinette apple from the previous year.

Where would she have gotten a warm, living child from? Asked the neighbours to lend her one? Or bought one at the market? Or swaddled up a baby lamb instead of a child?

Petrunia timidly pulled out her left breast from under her shirt, squeezed it with the two top fingers of her right hand, and then poked the pink nipple at the head of the "baby". The cold of the wrinkled apple-face made Petrunia's pink nipple become covered in tiny goose bumps.

As if embarrassed, Petrunia hastily tucked her breasts into her shirt, pushed the "baby" wrapped in burlap under the cushions and slowly got up off the bed.

That was it. She had fed the child. She felt better now.

Now she could go and feed the ravenous mawsof the cows and sheep, and talk to the restive bulls.

"LISTEN, VARVARCHUCHKA, has anyone passed on news from Ivan?" Oksena Prytuliak yelled over the fence early in the morning.

"No, there's been nothing," Petrunia lazily looked up from her vegetable patch, wiping her flushed forehead.

"Don't worry! There'll be news. I can tell," her neighbour placated her, having remembered before this to hang over the fence and to rummage about the yard with her eyes. "I waited a long time myself.You'll just have to be patient," Oksena surveyed the barn and stable one more time, and disappeared behind the gate on the far side of the road.

Petrunia was not worried. Whatever would be – would be. Ivan wasn't the only man who had gone off to fight. Half the village was fighting for the Kaiser. Oksena's husband Dmytro had finished fighting. The Russkies had taken him prisoner and were holding him in some place of theirs called Siberia. She had recently received a note from him.Her Dmytro was alive.

As for Petrunia, God forgive her, she didn't care one way or the other, whether her husband was alive or dead, whether birds had pecked out his eyes or he was rotting in some field, feeding the ravens.

To hell with it!

Whatever would be – would be.

If he was alive – she would meet him.

If he was dead – she would hold a church service for him.

But her eyes would never weep for him. That she knew for sure. But she dared not show anyone.

She went among the livestock in the most somber kerchiefs without flowers and remained silent more and more. She alone knew what was happening inside her heart.

93

Glory to God, she was healthy as an ox, so that she would live to see what God would send her. The work stopped her from thinking about Ivan. There was so much livestock bellowing in the stable and the cattle enclosure. So much live property milling before her eyes. Just try to look after them all!

But when in the space of a single week in her farmyard two cows had calved, a mare had foaled, and the sow had ten piglets, the yearling bull began to snort through his inflamed nostrils, like a bear in the brambles, and to scratch the stable floor so forcefully that sparks flew out from under the floorboards, and on the hay in the stable Petrunia was bitten on the leg by a weasel, young Varvarchuk's wife burst into tears for the first time, not out of pity for herself, but out of pity for the work that was beyond her strength.

She wept and slobbered, and then hobbled off to see her neighbours, the Cheviuks. To ask for help. Because there was no one else in the village she could turn to, lest they looked at her askance and cursed her as she left.

Kyrylo gave her his youngest son, Dmytryk.

Petrunia sighed with relief. She wouldn't have known what to talk about with Andriy. He was made for mischief, not work.

Meanwhile Dmytryk was practically a child. So kind and quiet. He said nothing and watched. He had big eyes. Bright eyes. In the corners of his lips there was a smile between two dimples. He was pure, like an angel. Innocent.

When she occasionally glanced across the road at the neighbouring household, where the Cheviuk's youngest son was splitting firewood, it sometimes occurred to Petrunia that she would rock that Dmytryk the way she secretly rocked her small child, and she would press his small white face to her breasts.

And Dmytryk was now quietly managing her household and looking after the Varvarchuk's livestock as if they were living people. He looked at Petrunia with his two starry eyes, without saying a word, but almost with devotion.

He was still very young.

Although Petrunia wasn't that far off his age herself.

"...MY GOD, PETRUNIA, WHAT'S THIS?" Dmytryk asked fearfully, smoothing out her white shirt covered with fresh traces of blood, while Petrunia made eyes at him, almost laughing, pressing her whole body against him, seeking his naked chest with her hot hand. "What is this?" the lad asked again in astonishment. As if he had just been struck by lightning.

"Blood," Petrunia answered simply and now covered her naked legs with a small *keptar*.

"What do you mean, blood?" the lad became perplexed for some reason and blushed terribly, so that even Petrunia became engulfed in a hot wave of shame.

"Yes. Blood. My virginal blood." Petrunia rose sluggishly from the bench and the delicious smell of freshly-rubbed late hay filled the nostrils of the two confused lovers.

"God, what have we done...?" Dmytryk said, tucking his naked legs under the hem of his long white shirt, grabbing hold of his head with both hands.

"What have we done, Dmytryk?!" Petrunia entwined herself around the confused lad, overjoyed, as if she had been hoisted upon a hundred horses at once. She rested her disheveled hair upon his knees. "What have we done?" she asked craftily, looking deep into his eyes.

"You've got a husband, and I..."

"I have a husband?!" she lifted her head sharply and rose to her knees, eye to eye with Dmytryk. "I have a husband??? He's no husband, he only torments me. Can't you see that?"

He sighed deeply:

"How can this be...?! I don't know what to do now."

Petrunia said nothing for a long time, only stroking Dmytryk's hair and from time to time kissed his almost childish face, covered in soft fluff.

"You don't need to do nothin'!" she almost yelled at him. "Just don't let me go back into the arms of that animal," she suddenly sobbed into the lad's chest, and he felt a cold tear rolling down his warm body.

Dmytryk shuddered and pressed the girlwoman close to himself. She couldn't stop crying and was choking on the words which had gathered in her throat.

"NO!" HAVRYLO DIACHUK YELLED into his son-in-law's eyes, holding a whip with an iron knob on the handle in one hand and supporting the white-faced Petrunia with the other. "No! I don't believe you! She was untouched!"

Ivan looked sullenly at his father-in-law, with a gaze like molten iron, and placed his hands on his hips like a woman about to launch into an argument, then finally burst out laughing:

"You don't believe me! Why don't you take a look! Go on!" and he pointed in the direction of the bed, covered with a green and beetroot-coloured Hutsul blanket. "Go on, take a look!" He tossed the blanket onto the floor and brought the white linen sheet almost up to Havrylo's eyes. "Take a look, mister Havrylo!"

Havrylo let go of his daughter's hand, tossed the whip onto the ground and with trembling hands smoothed out the sheet on the bed.

The sheet was white, because it was new, with white lace trim along the edges. Only in the middle did he see several dirty-yellow stains, as if someone had spat onto it and then tried to wipe away the spittle.

"Who?!" Havrylo attacked Petrunia with his fists, showering blows upon her head, shoulders and chest. "Tell me, you slut, who deprived you of your virginity, or I'll kill you right here and now!"

"That's right, have a talk with your daughter, mister farmer!" Varvarchuk slammed the door behind him so hard that it bounced back and closed again. Furious, he disappeared into the depths of the house.

Petrunia's disheveled hair whipped at her face, while her father's heavy hand lashed her back with the whip.

She barely defended herself, only sobbing from the pain and covering her face with her hands.

"Who deflowered you?" the father shook his daughter by the shoulders and struck her lips again with his open hand.

"He didn't deflower me..." Petrunia cried into her clenched fists, bent over double from the blow.

"Who did then?" another heavy fist straightened her.

"No one!" a black hatred burned in her eyes. "He didn't deflower me."

"What did he do with you then?"

Her face in tears, the daughter looked at her father with pitiful eyes, said nothing for a long time, and then whispered in a barely audible voice:

"He tormented me."

"But he has shamed me in front of the whole world!" Havrylo shook the whip in Petrunia's face. "He couldn't have lied!"

"He couldn't deflower me, because he can't get it up with women!" Petrunia was now yelling at her father. Such brazenness from his daughter made the father's eyes grow wider and wider. "But lie he could. And he lied to you about me!"

Petrunia wiped her tear-stained face with both hands, smoothed out her shirt, ripped open by the whip, and stood before her father in the hope that he would at last show her some pity.

"That doesn't matter now!" Havrylo yelled at his daughter and punched her in the face with all his might. "You're his wedded wife and you have to live with him. I've been shamed enough as it is." Havrylo took the whip in his other hand. "With a girl like you even a dead man could get it up. You're lying! But I'll find out who deprived you of your virginity, even if I die doing it!" he yelled and the metal knob on the whip handle came down on the girl's shoulders one final time.

...PETRUNIA PRESSED her "child" wrapped in silk cloth to her swollen breasts and bent over its "face" – soft tender words drifted barely audibly through the twilight in the room with drawn curtains.

Petrunia wanted to sing. But suddenly she bit her lips: she sensed someone was skulking outside under the windows. She hid the "child" under the cushions and sat still, without letting out a breath.

Someone was scratching at the window.

"Petrunia..." the glass whispered with the voice of Andriy Cheviuk. "Let me inside, Petrunia, or I'll smash the windows, if you don't... You know me!"

Reluctantly she unlocked the door and stood in the doorway, her arms folded across her chest.

"What do you want, neighbour?" Petrunia asked, without looking him in the eye.

"You know! I want what my brother's already had from you. But he doesn't know how to do it. I saw you two," Andriy twirled a white silk rope before her face, which was tied around the midriff of his long shirt embroidered with white thread.

"This is what I want. And don't you refuse me. No one refuses me. You're cold on your own in your bed. You have to stop seeing my brother, or I'll never ever forgive you this for all the money in the world. If you stay with me – you'll be all right. If you refuse – I'll take you all the same."

"Go home, Andriy, and stop trying to get bumped on the head." She closed the door in his face, and pressed herself against the wall.

Her heart was practically leaping out of her chest, but Petrunia pressed her left hand against it, and then placed her right hand on top as well.

For several months now Andriy was giving her no peace and promised to tell Ivan about her and Dmytryk when he returned from the war.

To hell with it! It was all the same to her. Whether that animal returned from the great slaughterhouse or not – her head did not ache over it. It would have been good if he were never to return. But she no longer knew how to hide her relationship with Dmytryk. Because they were enemies, her husband and her. Whichever way you looked at it – her husband was off at war. She had had enough shame. But she'd also had enough of that dungeon of a life with Ivan.

She couldn't tell people the truth. Anyway, they didn't want to know.

Petrunia stood before an icon, arms outstretched, like two doors opened wide, and her fingers wouldn't come together to say a prayer. She was incapable of praying to the Lord, or turning to Satan for help. For neither of them could help her. She had taken this path of her own free will.

And wordlessly Petrunia addressed her heart, as she had once addressed her Christian God. But even now she could not feel the shame of her situation. Nor any fear of Ivan. She was overcome by great joy, wrenched in two by grief and encroaching misfortune. Petrunia could sense with her prophetic heart that misfortune was drawing near.

...MARYNKA-GODSPIRIT stood in the Varvarchuk's yard, black as a nun in a long black skirt with a large black shawl thrown over a black bodice, holding a small bundle of yellow candles.

Petrunia dropped her pail of milk in surprise.

"Don't worry, daughter, I've come with a kind heart," Marynka said and made her way into the house. "I want to help you, or else misfortune may strike your home." She looked at Petrunia with gentle eyes, but suddenly wilted like a fallen leaf and tried to move the pots about in the oven.

"I want to charm your foolish heart. To put a spell on it, while people still aren't aware of anything. Because Dmytryk is pining after you and you are dying to be with him. But you two can't go on like this, children... You can't... something very bad may come of this..." Marynka spoke, as if she were lamenting, while Petrunia stood in the middle of the house like a sheaf of wheat, neither dead, nor alive, except that a sudden thought kept striking at her temples: 'How does she know that I'm dying after him?!'

"I know, my heart has eyes and it can see everything," Marynka seemed to read her thoughts and replied, sending wisps of aromatic smoke all around Petrunia. "When a heart loves it knows everything and hears everything without people ever saying a thing. Dmytryk is like my own child. He is Kyrylo's little baby. And I know everything about them, but I can't help any of them. My heart won't let me... But I can help you." Marynka began to take partly-burnt candles from her pocket, pieces of string, a poppy-seed head wrapped in a handkerchief and some matches.

"There's no need for that," Petrunia stopped her with her hand. "There's no need for that, Marynka. That won't help me. And I don't need any help."

"Oh!" Marynka threw both her arms up into the air. "You want him to kill you when he returns? He is already on his way home; he's already not far away. Can't you feel it?"

"It's all the same to me. There's not a drop of life left in me for him. All my life for Ivan has drained from me. He made it happen himself. And I don't care any more."

"Let me bewitch you," Marynka begged her, almost crying, and suddenly dropped to her knees before Varvarchuk's young wife. "I can do this only with your acquiescence. And I can help only you. My witchcraft can't help Dmytryk."

"No," Petrunia burst out with an almost evil laugh straight in the face of the blessed woman. "No, my silver Marynka. Get up. Your spells won't have any effect on me either. Because I don't want them to. Whatever will be - will be. I can't shrug off Dmytryk. And I don't care at all what that inhuman husband of mine does to me. He can't do any worse than he's done already. And if he does – then it's my fate. I'm not to blame. I am alive and I want to live."

"DMYTRYK... CAN YOU HEAR ME, Dmytryk..." she shook the sleepy lad by the shoulders. "Go home. It's night-time. Your mother will be worried about where you've gone."

"I told her that I was going out to hire some people for the mowing tomorrow," the lad replied, shaking the sleep from his head.

"You!" she slapped him on the chest, feigning anger. "Are you pretending to be asleep?"

"No. I really was asleep," he said, stretching both arms toward her.

"Go home. I can sense something bad."

"Andriy?"

"No."

"What then?"

"I don't know, but something bad will happen."

"Ivan..." the lad sighed and his hands dropped.

"Ivan..." Petrunia ground her teeth.

"I'll go and tell him myself..." Dmytryk tossed a handful of hay deep into the loft, trying to vent his anger.

"You won't manage. Andriy will beat you to it..." Petrunia said indifferently, and suddenly burst into tears so loudly and bitterly, that her weeping would have easily been heard outside the stable walls, had someone been standing there spying on them. "Make love to me, Dmytryk, one last time, because there will never be another time..." Petrunia said and, with a firm but trembling hand, pulled off first her shirt and then the boy's...

In the moonlight Andriy's shadow fell almost at their feet from the steps in the stable, but the couple, crazy with passion and despair, did not see him.

IVAN VARVARCHUK SAT on a flat stone outside the door to his house and watched the thick moonlight fill his backyard in the dead of night. An owl blinked from the walnut tree, the glint of its large eyes cold and creepy. Better that it had hooted. That might have stopped the ringing in Ivan's ears. Or maybe it could have pecked at his temples.

After leaving the inn, Ivan had thought that he was drunk, but now he wasn't sure whether he was drunk or had been made a laughing stock behind his back.

But today he was truly dead. The cannons hadn't killed him at the front, but two steps from home he had been knifed in the heart.

However, even as dead as he was, with the blood drained from his veins, he was afraid to knock at his own door.

Dear people...

He had returned from the war!

And his wife had been making love to another man in his house!

Meanwhile he was afraid to slam one fist against the door and the other into his wife's ribs.

Because he didn't believe Andriy.

If the Jew's wife Fira had whispered to him about Petrunia's sins, he would have believed her from the second word. But when the Cheviuk's stallion had recounted the story, he seemed to be afraid of his own words.

And with whom, pray tell?! A child? A snotty-nosed lad?

Would she have let anyone come near her after everything that had transpired?

As for that... well, the thing that made many a sensible fellow lose his head, Petrunia had no interest in that, because she didn't know what it was about. She knew how to bake bread, how to weave and sew, how to dry hay and to bring a cow to a bull.

But what Ivan didn't need her to know, she knew nothing about. Well, the fact that she hadn't known anything before him, or with him – that he could vouch for.

But why did she need to know, if Ivan didn't know himself? Couldn't a person live without this?

My oath one could! How well he had managed without this bit of foolishness for so long! Only at the front had he cursed his fate, for he was very scared of death from a bullet or a cannon. And when the men laughed at him, accusing him of saving his seed for his wife – that didn't make him feel any better.

The fact that Ivan's mother had given birth to him like this, that meant God had meant him to be like he was. Such men were needed too, if they were born into this world, created by the hand of the Lord.

That his wife really was untouched to this day, after all these years of marriage – who was to know that? That was an intimate matter. Not for strangers to be privy to. However, she feared Ivan and would never lose that fear. Ivan would have let his head be chopped off in order to prove that this was the holy truth. Petrunia remembered only too well her father's whip upon her shoulders. And she would never break her oath to Ivan – never.

Oh, ye-e-s... There had been a time... there had been a time when Ivan had been forced to kiss the earth and ask the Lord's forgiveness for his treatment of Petrunia: when at the front they had been fired on by cannons from one side and a cloud of gas had drifted over from the other side, released onto their army by their allies, the Germans. Their allies could have poisoned them all, instead of the Russians. The Krauts didn't know that the front had been breached and that the Austrian units had also entered into the Russkies' rear. And to this day Ivan was coughing up that German poison as a result, while many of his comrades-in-arms had succumbed to the gas attack.

It was then, when his insides were being emptied and he felt he was dying, that Ivan remembered his wedding day. It was then that he cursed his fields and livestock, for the sake of which he had married the hard-working and soft-spoken Petrunia.

He had lied to Havrylo about his daughter's chastity – what was so heartless about that? In these mountains a girl was more afraid of her husband, than her father. But she also dared not contradict her husband, even when he was lying.

What was Ivan to do otherwise? Tell his father-in-law that he was impotent?! That he could not satisfy his wife?

What man could continue living with such a shame?

Ivan had to show his father-in-law his daughter's blood, to prove his male virility.

But since Petrunia didn't understand anything about how a man and a woman did it, that wasn't so bad.

Had he owned up about his impotence to Havrylo, his father-in-law would never have taken his daughter back anyway: no farmer would have exchanged Ivan's real estate for his daughter's honour. But would any man in the world, finding himself in Ivan's predicament, have admitted to his shame?!

Never once had Petrunia spoken with Ivan about the problem. She would lie down in bed, be it summer or winter, and would talk with Ivan about any old thing, but she never breached this subject.

Nor spoke about having been insulted. Nor about her life with Ivan devoid of any kind of embracing or love-making.

Nor did Ivan mention anything.

What for?

The cows calved.

The sheep lambed.

The pigs farrowed.

The bulls inseminated.

What else did she need?

In their old age the Varvarchuks would take in some fosterling, so that there would be someone to close their eyes in death. But for now it was good, there were no additional worries.

Did he lock the storeroom from his wife?

Didn't he buy her kerchiefs from the Vyzhnytsia Jews?

Until Ivan had been taken off to war, they had lived nicely, making all the old women around envy them their wealth.

And no one had given them a helping hand either.

What people had gossiped about after the wedding – it had been about Petrunia and her father. As for Ivan, Ivan was a farmer. Ivan should be kissed on the backside for his wealth, instead of needing to put up with his wife's pouting.

He still couldn't understand why Andriy had told him about Petrunia and Dmytryk! He had probably lied out of envy. He was the type of fellow who would not relent until he got his way with a woman. And he must have been slapped on the wrists by Petrunia.

For Ivan was sure of his wife.

...PETRUNIA SEEMED TO TAKE TOO LONG to open the door, she clattered with the yew bolt for a long time, however she finally opened the door so sharply, that Ivan barely managed to avoid being hit.

She did not fall upon his chest – but he never expected as much.

Saying no word, she lit two lamps for some reason, and Varvarchuk thought that she must have been overjoyed that her husband had finally returned. Alive. Unharmed.

She was definitely pleased, because over there the white bed linen was spread out.

Strange! She was sleeping on the bed, instead of on the oven.

And she didn't have an ordinary nightshirt on, but one with white lace.

"I've returned from the war," was the first thing Varvarchuk said to his wife. "And I'm going to bed now. We can talk tomorrow." He grabbed her by the hand and dragged her off to bed.

He felt her resistance for only a slight moment. A fleeting moment. Then she obediently lay down up against the wall and Ivan lay facing her. His rough hand slowly followed the contours of her body over the shirt from her head to her feet and back to her head, and her skin became covered with goose-bumps: she had never felt Ivan's hand on her body.

...Two months later Ivan sat down on a stool in the middle of the room and made Petrunia get down on her knees before him.

"Swear that you were faithful to me!"

She looked him in the eye, then ran her eyes from his head to his feet.

He felt as if she had thrown a handful of hot ashes in his eyes.

As if she had pierced him with a bolt of lightning or impaled him on a stake.

She looked insolently at her husband, and then spoke brazenly and boldly:

"I swore an oath to you before the people and the Lord in church. I did not break my oath. What is there to swear now? You are my wedded husband. You have the right to check if I have been faithful to you. You never deflowered me. So if you want to know, whether I was loyal, take me. Right now, if you like."

Her voice at once bore so much irreverence and arrogance, so much despair and naked triumph, and her body had bloomed, holding real female power, making Varvarchuk feel giddy.

However he did not reply. He only forbade her to venture beyond the gate to their yard. She was to sit at home, and if she went to church or anywhere else, she could only go in his company.

And yet Petrunia never stared at the gate. Wordlessly she only skulked between the house, the stable, the storehouse, the well, the threshing barn and the cellar.

But when one day Varvarchuk spied his wife atop the haystack with her hand against her forehead gazing at the Cheviuk's household, and Dmytryk was doing the same from there, he immediately set off for Hrytsko Keyvan's place. Even though they had fought during the war in different areas, a soldier always understood another, especially when it came to such matters.

HRYTSKO KEYVAN didn't take much notice of Ivan's words. In silence he riveted his scythe in the orchard and occasionally glanced at the cowering Ivan.

Varvarchuk had dashed off to Keyvan's place like a young stallion, bounding over neighbour's property lines. A black fury was wrenching his chest apart – he felt like tearing it out of himself, the way one pulled out that first grey hair from one's head.

But when the two dark twin boys raced joyously from Keyvan's gate, followed by Teofila, Keyvan's morose wife, who pitter-pattered after them like a mother hen, greeting Ivan with her head held low, Varvarchuk's previous resolve disintegrated.

He leaned against the fence and watched Hrytsko skillfully wield a mandrel and a hammer.

Had Ivan remained standing there for a minute or two longer he could have returned home without even uttering a 'hello'.

"May the Lord help you!" Varvarchuk greeted Keyvan at that moment and stepped onto the mown grass under the walnut tree.

Keyvan raised his head, shaded by a green hat, smiled into his moustache, which was twirled upward, and replied:

"Thank you. May the Lord help you too! I haven't seen you in public for a long time, soldier..." Hrytsko said, without distracting himself from his chore. "There's holy Sunday, festive days, and you keep attending to your livestock and your wife, as if you can't take your eyes off them. Never time to drop in on an old comrade-in-arms and to remember the days spent in the trenches, to have a drink in memory of fallen comrades... Oh, Ivan..." Ivan remained silent and scratched his head. And then, without beating about the bush, he said:

"I've come to hire you, Hrytsko, to help me with a very delicate matter. Any other fellow would refuse me. But I know that you can't… Leave that scythe alone and let's talk man to man…"

"… I'M OFF TO HUSK the maize."

Petrunia wrapped her head in a dark kerchief, tied an apron around her waist and went into the entrance hall without closing the door behind her.

Ivan watched her feet move up the rungs of the ladder limply and lazily. As if weights had been tied to them.

Slowly and unwillingly, as if being forced to do so, her right hand dragged the wicker basket up with her.

And it made him want to howl.

To trample his wife with his feet.

But now there was nothing to trample her for.

Ivan struck the table with his fist.

Petrunia's soft cat-like steps echoed through the attic.

He knew that she had moved the wooden stool closer to the window,

laid out the dry maize cobs all around her,

placed the basket on her knees –

and from under her fingers fell the yellow gold of the maize kernels.

But he also knew that her eyes, swifter that her hands, were unblinkingly fixed on Pavlo Cheviuk's yard. There Dotsia had brought out Dmytryk, with one of the children helping her, into the orchard. She lay him in the shade under the walnuts, wrapped in a woolen carpet or a *dzherha*[27], and went off to take care of her endless house duties, returning from time to time either with a mug of milk or a bowl of warm *borsch*[28].

Dotsia fed Dmytryk, then stroked his forehead, and returned to her chores.

Meanwhile, without stopping to husk the detested maize, Petrunia swallowed tears in the attic, listening in case Ivan crept up the stairs.

And so they lived, each with their own truth and their own torment.

To this day Ivan wasn't sure whether Andriy had lied to him about Petrunia and Dmytryk. He might not have believed him. But the unheard-of audacity that his quiet, intimidated Petrunia had displayed, the naked challenge she had confronted him with: 'Why don't you deflower me, then you'll know whether I was faithful or not!', awakened such a rush of anger in him, that afterwards he stood under the pelting water of a waterfall many a time to cool the fire in his brain. Back then he was even capable of killing his own father.

If back then, on the festival of Ivan Kupalo, Dmytryk had denied any wrongdoing or Petrunia had interceded on his behalf, if they had begged him forgiveness, gotten down on their knees, blood would have clouded Ivan's eyes in rage – and after that the village priest would have had two jobs at the cemetery to attend to.

But both of them had remained silent.

After Dmytryk's last rib had cracked under Keyvan's feet – only then had Ivan grabbed hold of his head and thought: what if young Cheviuk had lied?

---

27   *Dzherha* – dialectical word for a multicolored Hutsul woolenblanket.

28   A traditional Ukrainian beetroot soup.

What if he should have beaten up Andriy instead of his younger brother?!

...Ivan struck the table with his fist with even greater rage. He had no power over his wife. Not a crumb, not a gramme, even if he were to lock her in the cellar. There wasn't enough work for her down there to justify her staying there all day. Even in the cellar there was an air vent through which his wife's soul could float outside and into the Cheviuk's yard under the walnuts!

"...AND NOW YOU CAN kill me too, just like you killed him..." Petrunia told Ivan indifferently, watching the people emerge from Pavlo's front gate after the wake.

Ivan said nothing in reply. He only felt that everything that was alive inside him had exploded.

In the evenings he sat on the threshold of his house and for some reason thought about Hrytsko Keyvan, rather than Dmytryk.

And only afterwards did his thoughts turn to Petrunia. He was ready to watch a stranger's coarse hand feel up his wife in his presence.

But in their village such hands had probably long since withered or had yet to be born.

Ivan even wanted someone to say something about his wife – either good or bad.

But in Tysova Rivnia people would talk longer about a bull which had failed to inseminate a cow, than about some person, especially when that person was Petrunia.

Finally the time arrived when people even stopped asking the Varvarchuks to various celebrations and no longer expected them in church.

For some reason even the omnipresent Gypsies avoided their large and imposing house, the gates of which now stood half-opened.

...THE AGEING PETRUNIA entered the large guest room each day, locked the door from the inside with a bolt and pulled her tiny "baby" out of the chest from under all the rags beneath which it was buried.

These days the "baby" was made of Dmytryk's white shirt, left behind by him in the hay above the stable on that night when Ivan Varvarchuk was returning from the war and dropped into the Jewish inn with Andriy Cheviuk.

The shirt linen of the "baby" was aged and yellowed, just like Petrunia's face.

But she failed to notice this. Her rough, wrinkled hands caressed the saffron-yellow "face" of her never conceived, unborn baby, and her wrinkled face pressed against the old bundle of cloth, sniffing it all over. And from there, from the depths of the years and her memory, she recalled the familiar and indestructible scent of an impassioned man's body, mixed with the fragrance of trampled late hay and salty sweat, ripe apples and fresh milk, the smell of a young lamb's skin and the smell of slippery male seed spilled upon her white loins.

Petrunia kept the "baby" on her knees and looked out the window for a prolonged moment of time, without blinking. There a smiling healthy young Dmytryk stood and watched her with such innocent and bewildered eyes, that Petrunia again pressed herself against his shirt "baby", gritting her teeth till they ached, so as not to scream.

Petrunia closed her eyes – and from the attic window, where she husked the damned maize, no longer of any use to her, she could see Dmytryk, barely able to

113

move, lying in Pavlo's orchard under the walnuts, trying to raise himself ever so slightly on his elbow.

Dotska was fussing around him. Then she dashed into the house and returned with an armful of pillows, with which she gingerly propped up Dmytryk's shoulders and without rushing, as if her feet were tired, she returned to her chores.

The lad was utterly exhausted, but with an almighty effort he hoisted himself up on his right hand, and with his left hand resting on his heart, waved almost imperceptibly to Petrunia with his small yellow palm.

He could always sense when she was looking in his direction.

When she was standing in her yard facing in his direction.

When she tripped over the rock returning from the well with full buckets.

When she was weeping in the cellar, her face buried in the fragrant reinette apples, taking bites out of them, as she had once taken bites out of her insane joy in the hay above the stable.

Dmytryk then breathed at her.

From every little crack.

With every breath of wind.

With every leaf.

Every drop of rain.

But what of it?

Petrunia kissed her "baby" one last time and slowly untwisted the shirt. For a long time she caressed the shirt's old linen, as if her hand was a hot iron. Then she lovingly folded the shirt and placed it in the very bottom of the chest. Pressing it down flat with her hand.

Thus she had nailed her heart to the bottom of her memory, having paid for her fleeting joy with the life of an innocent soul.

Petrunia tied a black kerchief over the red one.

She put on a summer *keptar*.

Slid a candle into her bosom.

And for the first time in many years she ventured outside the gate without Ivan's permission.

Her walk was heavy.

Her head even heavier.

But she was unable to stop herself any longer.

For the first time in all these years Petrunia was sitting alone at the foot of Dmytryk's grave and the tears flowed freely down her wilted face furrowed with wrinkles.

She did not wipe the tears away and did not look about to see if anyone was in the cemetery. She didn't care.

Even if her equally infirm Ivan were to find his way here now (the devil had not taken him yet!) with a whip in his hand.

Even if all the Cheviuks were to start throwing rocks at her, none of them, save Andriy, having the slightest idea of her trespass against their family.

Petrunia pressed her face against the grave and, weeping, kissed the dry earth.

Meanwhile, Dotska stood nearby, all hunched over, wringing her hands and casting furtive glances in all directions to make sure Ivan was nowhere to be seen. Her shrunken body was shaking, because it seemed to her that even now, after all these years, old Varvarchuk had

not yet settled his score with Dmytryk over Petrunia.
That was the type of person Ivan was.
And anyway, people never manage to thank
others for their good deeds, or to pay
them back for their insults.
Not anyone. Not even themselves.
And it is hardly ever
otherwise.

PART THREE

THE SWING OF LIFE

MARYNKA-GODSPIRIT WAS RHYTHMICALLY pushing an empty swing tied to an ancient old pear tree with ropes – and the pear tree, like a person wearied by life, obediently and unfailingly creaked in time to its unhurried sweeps: *'hoyda… hoy-da'*. The dried, cracked planks of the swing's seat, nailed to two perpendicular cross-members, creaked too, barely supported by the ropes, which had become frayed by the elements and time. They barely kept the home-made swing attached to the pear tree.

Brave morning shafts of sunlight broke through the leaves into the shade of the orchard, where the cold of the night still lingered. Bees buzzed at the tops of their voices and there was a sharp smell of young mint.

In the adjacent yard a colt was neighing excitably, set off by someone's smell, as if competing with the shrill bleating of sheep let out to graze before dawn.

"Hi-ta-a-ah… hi-ta-a-ah…" Marynka purred to herself and pushed the swing ever higher into the very top of the pear tree.

Marynka usually rocked alone on the swing, while the people of Tysova Rivnia tended their livestock and hoed their vegetable patches, without giving their tongues free rein, so as not to waste time.

For Marynka this daily swinging did more for her than washing and having breakfast. She would jump to her feet before sunrise, no matter whether it was summer or winter, splash some cold water over her face, chew on a freshly-picked sour cherry leaf or a stem of mint or squash a few frozen guelder-rose berries in her mouth, and then silently make herself comfortable on the swing, always first spreading an old woolen shawl over the seat.

Marynka would not have exchanged this shawl, left her by her maternal granny, Fedora, for any dowry. Because Fedora's shawl was alive. Marynka took it in her hands – and after a short while she could hear the shawl communicating with her. No-no, not through words: the shawl passed on its ardour through Marynka's palms. Through her palms she received prophetic words from the shawl, which then created utter confusion in Marynka's innocent head.

People lied when they said that her great-grandmother had practised shamanism or *molfarstvo*, as the Hutsuls called it, and that she herself had inherited the gift, passed on from generation to generation. Marynka laughed at such talk. What shamanism?

Fortune-telling involved collecting magic herbs from a certain place at a certain time;

then mixing and stirring them, roasting them over a fire;

one stole things from dead bodies,[29]

and made potions from them,

and then befuddled people's minds.

That was shamanism.

But she knew nothing about such sorcery.

Marynka did not tell fortunes – she had knowledge.

But only while she was swinging on this swing,

and only when she was wrapped in her great-grandmother's shawl.

---

29 The Hutsuls have an ancient custom of fortune telling using certain items taken from a dead person. For example, in the villages there are women who "specialize" in stealing things from dead people: tearing off pieces of clothing in which the dead person is dressed, removing the rope with which the deceased person's legs are bound (to keep them together). A piece of a deceased person's clothing is considered a special lucky charm (the Hutsuls call it an *oberih* or *zastupnyk*) to be used by a family in times of disaster or illness. Such "lucky charms" are believed to guard family members and their home from lightning, protect cattle against misfortune, etc. (author)

Only then did God reveal things to her.

She had lots of swings all over the place across these boundless mountains – but only one spoke to her, this one beside her house.

Once Kyrylo had made swings for Marynka throughout Bochkiv, beside practically every path. He would debark three or four young maple or ash saplings, bind them together, then fix rope or wild grape vines to each end and attach them to a young fir tree or beech – and he pushed Marynka's swing up to the heavens, making her catch her breath, it was so frightening! And then he sat on the ground, pressed his face against Marynka's knees and kept whispering something to her... and whispering... and then proceeded to caress her knees... and utter marvelous words... as if he was placing a spell on her.

She went completely deaf then, hearing only the blood pounding in her temples and pumping into her heart. And that foolish heart clattered away for all it was worth, pushing Marynka into Kyrylo's embraces. Barely conscious, as if drugged with roseroot, she slid down to the ground – and the two of them tumbled into the moss or leaf mould. Their lips rustled because of the heat of day, dryly sliding across lips and face; urgent hands chased one another, as if competing which of them would first seize the other and press hardest against them; their eyes grew blind from the unseen splendour of sounds and smells, as well as the shameless nakedness of each other's young body.

And after both had played about until they were exhausted, after they had caught their breath and napped a little in the shade, Kyrylo, if he still had time, would weave her a swing out of wild grapevine. He would sit, resting his back against a tree-trunk, whistling some wedding ditty, and adroitly work his fingers.

And lo and behold – in a moment the swing flew high above the treetops, bearing Marynka into the sky, and the ever more beautiful young lass yelled joyously into the surrounding silence, and rejoiced at her ineffable happiness.

"Will you make our children a cradle like this too?" Marynka asked, getting in Kyrylo's way with her kisses and hugs.

"You are my princess…" Kyrylo would reply seriously. "The best weavers will weave my princess a cradle. And I'll just make swings for you. And push you upon them myself. No one is allowed to push the swing of the princess, except for the prince himself."

Oh, swinging her… He swung her over onto her back in the hay in Ivantsio's cottage, as if he was indeed twirling her about on a swing – and the Earth parted beneath her. Except that it didn't swallow her up, for the Earth too must have taken pity on Marynka's heart, which again burst at the seams with joy and languor. Ahoy! Where was that swing which had swung and rocked her heart like a bell, and did not stop, did not slow down – only inflaming her further, just as Kyrylo was lighting a fragrant little fire in the middle of the cottage over there and a summer thunderstorm was raging upon the wooden shingles on the roof.

But a horned owl was screeching somewhere in the crown of a beech tree.

And some departed person's irreconcilable little soul was brushing against the outside walls of the cottage.

As if spying on them.

Or warning them of some misfortune.

Or threatening the secret lovers.

But this only peppered their blood even more with the spice of danger and passion.

121

Nothing more.

Sin?!

When both of them had lost their heads in Ivantsio's hay, hadn't it been all the same to Marynka whether there had been bridesmaids or a master-of-ceremonies at their side?!

She felt she had grabbed the Lord Himself by the beard.

Because Kyrylo's arm was pulling her toward him with such devilish power that she was incapable of refusing him or resisting him.

Even if she were to be stoned to death or burnt at the stake the following day – she would ask that they first let her have a swing. On the swing behind Ivantsio's cottage, where Kyrylo was now crucifying her with his hot hands, as if he wanted to remove her heart from her bosom, the same way he had often removed trembling blind baby birds from their nests.

Oh-o-o-oh-oh… Marynka had hanged herself on that swing in Bochkiv. She had cut one end of the grapevine with a knife and tied it around her neck, and tried to hang herself from the beech tree that it was attached to.

But as they say: what's given in this life will not happen in death. God had not wanted to accept Marynka's soul and the grapevine broke.

Did it matter what Kyrylo had told her after that?! Not at all! The important thing was that he had told her the truth. He was marrying Vasylyna for her land and mountain pastures laden with sheep.

And the rest… bah… it didn't matter.

And a week before his wedding Kyrylo chopped down and burnt every single one of the swings he had built for Marynka.

She had run from one terrifying forest bonfire to another, as if visiting people who had lost everything in a fire.

She fell upon the blackened earth.

Beat her head against it.

Screamed.

Entwined her arms around beech trees.

Stood upon anthills.

Everything around her breathed so full of life – only Marynka kept dying, and then reviving, until she sensed that the heart inside her had finally died. She placed her hands to her bosom, but there was no heart there. Marynka's heart did not beat during the day, or during the night – as if it had indeed escaped from her without trace. But no one had hidden it and no one grieved over it. Even she herself did not know where it had gone.

And from that time on she lived without a heart.

Perhaps she was able to hear others, because her heart did not get in the way?

…Then Marynka's face became dark and she returned to the mountains with the bluish mark around her neck left by the wild grapevine – and in two days collected all the ash from her swings into a kerchief and dug it into the ground next to the wall of Ivantsio's cottage. There, where until recently her heart had been turning to ash next to Kyrylo's.

And a handful of the grey ash she buried in her orchard under the pear tree.

After a while she made herself a swing.

The first time she settled on the boards of the new swing in her orchard, a frightful coldness shot all the way up to her brain. Marynka cowered, but did not get off her swing. As if waiting for the fear to pass.

However, the fear did not subside; in fact, it nailed her harder to the swing. Then she felt cold pins and needles in her feet, and her arms became powerless. And then, from both below and above she felt a breath of cold air. This was a deathly cold, mixed with deathly fear. She felt as if she were walking through a cemetery at night. And then fear itself, rather that her numb arm, tore her great-grandma Fedora's woolen shawl off her shoulders and spread it over the seat of the swing.

It was then that she had her first revelation.

At first Marynka was amazed when heat began to rise from beneath the shawl through her body. A burning-hot heat, as if she had sat down on a red-hot frying-pan. No, not even a frying-pan – she felt someone was threading a flaming-hot stake through her, like a thread being threaded through the eye of a needle… as if her body was being wound around a sharp-tipped tree trunk, sharp as a hunter's pickaxe.

Marynka barely stopped herself from screaming – the burning heat was spreading through her head in strange images… images which turned into people… people whom she recognized…

But then she did let out a scream – making the swing tremble. Fear sliced through Marynka's body: living people whom she knew, people who had greeted her only the day before, were suddenly dead… no-no, they still walked past her gate, she still exchanged words with them from her swing, but she could already see their sudden death before her eyes or their impending misfortune.

Strangely enough Marynka soon recovered. Things happened… The day before she went to bed, having said only a brief "Lord's Prayer", instead of separately thanking God for the day and the food, the weather and her good health. And only the day before she had cursed the neighbour's chickens to high heaven for having scratched her vegetable patch clean of everything.

But strange visions did not leave her the next day either – and Marynka struck her forehead full force with her hand. Well, yes… obviously it was right… how could she have it otherwise?! She was guilty before the Lord, for she herself had raised her hand against a life which had been granted by Him! She had wanted death for herself – but the Lord had given her life, for some reason refusing to accept Marynka's crushed soul. She had committed an unredeemable sin. God was now frightening her with these frightful visions. He was teaching her not to interfere with Him.

That day Gypsies from Storozhynets wandered through the village and Marynka exchanged her festive Easter shirt, embroidered with white roses on white linen, for a cast iron cauldron from them.

She now kept the pot-bellied vat behind the threshing barn. She reminded herself of her sin or scared people with hell. For she was about to do something unusual: at dawn she wanted to boil tar in the cauldron. She made the bottom red-hot and then tossed in a chunk of solidified tar. It was like throwing a rock into water. The damned chunk cracked from the extreme heat and began to bubble madly for all nearby to hear. The stench permeated everything. It smelt as if human bones were bubbling away in that cauldron. And it filled people's hearts with terror. And made them stop and think. As if to say: 'Look what will become of you, good folk, if you start thinking stupid things and acting stupidly. You'll burn in hell like this tar in the cauldron. And only foul smoke will emanate from your unclean bodies.'

Marynka watched the boiling black mass in the cauldron, hot and ugly, and terror entered her body, impregnating it to the very marrow inside her bones. Even through her tightly-shut eyes she imagined the smoke rising from her body in the hellish black melting pot – and she wanted to yell for the whole world to hear that she was innocent. It was not because of Kyrylo, not because of her newly found ability to prophesy.

Had she known that it would be like this… but no! All the same she would have acted exactly the same way. No! Not the same way! She would have loved Kyrylo even more. So that she could have loved her fill. Or she would have had a child by him. Who cared if people pointed their fingers at her and called her a slut?

She had removed the hot blood from her heart – and no longer feared death.

She had turned her heart into ash, wrenched it from her bosom like a shard of glass, and now went about with her insides slashed open, except that nobody noticed her open wound.

'They're not talking to me,' thought Marynka, when someone stopped to address her, 'they're staring into an open grave in which my blood has been laid to rest, because they want to take a good look at how a person can endure this life without blood or a heart. They want to gaze their fill at a dead soul.'

But another thought struck Marynka: whoa there, woman! No one knows about your sin with Kyrylo. Everything has long since been covered in ash. It has frozen over, like this almost iron-like piece of tar, which can't be smashed, not even with an axe. But smash it she had to. And she tossed it into the vat. To warn others against doing what she herself did not dare enunciate.

At first the neighbours were angry with her. They thought Marynka had forever taken leave of her senses. But at times she came out into the street, stood there awhile and looked about, then asked a passer-by to return home because a piece of good news was awaiting them there, and told them that if they continued on – there would be only bad news. Or else she came to someone's home, ostensibly for a drink of water, and stood there and thought a while and then convinced the wife not to send her child to the meadow that day to tend the cows. And that evening news spread through the village that a bull had attacked some shepherd on the pasture, and someone's child had been gored to death.

And one time the most important thing was revealed to Marynka: she knew exactly what would happen to each person in their village the following day. But for some strange reason the knowledge excluded Kyrylo and his family. And after that she felt good. She did not suffer with the knowledge of bad things about to happen to the person who nearly sent her packing into the other world. Let the man rejoice, if the Lord had granted him pleasure. Kyrylo had earned his pleasure. And his children too.

God would judge the rest.

And Marynka would be punished for the lot of them.

For what else was there for her to do in this world, when the world had taken all work away from her, except for one task – to know other people's misfortune and to suffer it on their behalf.

... *FROM DAWN MARYNKA* pushed her swing, but refused to sit on it herself. Something was not quite right on this day. Ever since nightfall a very distant and very strong force had been rocking the ground under the whole village, as if a multitude of horsemen were racing along and the ground shook under them – but no one else sensed this, except perhaps for the neighbour's anxious young horse, and Marynka. The bees didn't count. Bees were stupid – they drank blossom, shed honey, and sensed no alarm. But Marynka did. From early morning her hands had been shaking slightly and she felt a cold sensation under her breasts. And so she sat motionless beside her swing, talking to it, but not daring to look up.

Unease sucked at her breasts... a child must suck at its mother's teats like this... something bad was rising in her bosom, like a snake crawling along a warm summer path.

Marynka sensed a fire unfolding in her insides. She wanted to extinguish it. But with what? She couldn't be bothered fetching water. And her feet had become rooted to the ground beneath the pear tree. She could not hear a single living soul nearby. And even if she had heard someone – she wouldn't have moved from her spot or let out a peep: some devilish force was rocking the ground under her ever more forcefully – until the swing itself had become caught in the crown of the pear tree and swung like a dead body above her head. Marynka began to shudder, as if she had a fever. And she left the orchard without having pulled the swing free.

She already knew that a fire was heading for Tysova Rivnia. People were being tossed about before her burning eyes – but she only covered her face with her palms, as if trying to protect herself from the flames.

Marynka saw that she would be able to save herself.

But not other people.

And, what a miracle! All of Kyrylo's family passed before her glazed eyes. They dashed past her like a lightning bolt. And disappeared. The Cheviuks left behind only a long thin trail of flame – which melted away somewhere over Boznia or Bochkiv, swirling up into the sky in a thin white wisp of smoke.

What was all that about?!

...*AND BEFORE MIDDAY* the church bells began to toll.

Three times, and then three times more.

This was the customary way of notifying local villagers about approaching fires, calling on the male farmers to grab empty buckets and spades and run for all they were worth to the place from which the smoke was billowing.

Hearing the urgent tolling, Hrytsko Keyvan nimbly climbed the walnut tree behind the stable, almost like a youth, and from there he could see the whole flat part of the village, as well as the densely sown surrounding hilltops and gullies.

As usual, people's cattle grazed here and there, from time to time merrily jingling their bells.

Here and there on the light patches of hillsides, covered in mown grass, people were raking up hay, yelling at horses, which lazily dragged the round heaps of grass to the haystacks; or else they simply called out to each other from hilltop to hilltop, greeting equally tired mowers and rakers.

Shouting loudly to one another, the men sharpened their scythes.

The womenfolk replied, laughing at the men's jokes.

And only the echo lazily deflected the human voices into the grey mist of distant summits and peaks.

But this day, alongside the muffled echo, the surrounding summer stillness was split by the tolling bell from the valley – whilst the people in the highlands and lowlands disconcertedly turned their heads in the direction of the village church, which had suddenly come alive.

Hrytsko Keyvan also twisted his head about up in the walnut tree, looking for smoke above the village houses. But there was no smoke at all above any of the houses. Only a pillar of dust slowly began to rise along the main village road because of people's hasty footsteps, summoned to church by the unexpected tolling.

Meanwhile the bell began to toll continuously and, after hesitating for a short moment whether to take buckets or not, Hrytsko hoisted a shovel on his shoulder and, without closing his gate, gave free reign to his legs.

There was an unusual hubbub in the middle of the village – for on this occasion the women had assembled with the men for some reason, abandoning their work and their children, not even covering their heads properly with kerchiefs. The initial excitement, provoked by the sudden unease, was slowly subsiding – and at once it became quiet outside the church, as if a body was about to be displayed.

The hushed people waited for the village elder.

The Tysova Rivnia chief, the courteous landholder Vasyl Krylchuk, arrived at the church, accompanied by Hans Kruger, the leader of the local gendarmerie. Both were somewhat anxious, although they tried hard not to show it.

Despite no order being given, the village men surrounded them in a tight circle, pushing the women aside, and whispered among themselves.

At last Kruger spoke. His speech was soft. People hardly understood anything. But his first words were clearly not those of a military man:

"People! I don't have good news for you. But speak I must, for a war is approaching."

The leader of the local gendarmes heaved a deep sigh and spoke briefly and anxiously, which made his words even less comprehensible:

"The peaceful political relations between the Austrian crown and Serbia are coming to an end. The Kaiser's government has been forced to issue Serbia an ultimatum. Our border with Russia is also experiencing tension. There is a possibility that the Russian side is committing unfriendly actions, including military strikes. Incidents of sabotage have already been reported in various districts of our land. In the case of the slightest suspicion of collaboration by the civilian population with the enemy, such actions will be judged exclusively by military tribunals.

Therefore our Excellency the Kaiser and I, as the representative of his military administration, warn each of you at this dangerous time for our land, against making rash statements and committing indiscreet actions, which might be viewed as undermining the crown."

Kruger cleared his throat, took another deep breath, ran his tired gaze over the subdued people and continued:

"By the power invested in me I hereby bring to your attention that on this day the Kaiser has announced a general mobilization in defence of the land. All men born between 1 January 1872 and 31 December 1895 are obliged to carry out their civil duty and enroll in the Landsturm[30]. The Landsturm troops will depart today to a designated place, of which they will be informed separately.

---

30 The *Landsturm*, a German word for third-class infantry, were irregular military forces in Austria during WW1, called on to defend the country.

And the civilian population will have to maintain their vigilance and calm. Unlawful possession of firearms will be punished by summary execution. Those caught bearing firearms will be similarly dealt with."

...The year was 1914, three days before the feast of the Prophet Elijah[31].

...*KEYVAN'S TEOFILA WAS PLANTING* garlic for the winter when her neighbour, Kateryna Vasylashchuk, short of breath from the brisk walking, suddenly bent over the woman's ear and fervently whispered for the whole yard to hear:

"Did ya hear, Filya? Some of the men are coming back from the war. They say yours is not far away either. He was seen in Vashkivtsi today. Just so that you're prepared." The neighbour went silent for a brief moment, and then suggested in a somewhat conspiratorial tone: "But before he appears, my darling Filya, you should send your children off to your mum's." And she wrung her hands, as if she was about to burst into tears.

Teofila also had reason to wring her hands. But she didn't. She merely placed the remainder of the garlic bulbs at the edge of the garden bed and shook her hands free of dirt even more slowly. Only then did she feel a sharp pain under her left breast and then a treacherous languor spread through her body.

"Thank the Lord Jesus Christ that they are returning alive and well," she answered Mrs. Vasylashchuk and made her way into the house, not wishing to continue the conversation.

Her neighbour only shrugged her shoulders. And crossed herself silently. And pitter-pattered back home across the street.

31   The church festival of the prophet Elijah is on 2 August (20 July according to the old Julian calendar). Common folk considered this to be the start of autumn.

No sooner did Teofila cross the threshold to her house, than she began to pace from wall to wall, the way an animal darts about when it finds itself in a hunter's trap.

She tore at her hair.

Beat her head with her fists.

Tried to squeeze sobs from her chest.

And she dropped onto the bench against the wall and suddenly her head was released from despair. Why fight it now? Why sob? She should hasten to prepare herself for death before her husband arrived home from the war.

From that moment everything began to burn in the unfortunate woman's hands; apart from her imminent end, she could think of nothing else: neither her children, nor other people's judgment, nor pangs of conscience or sins.

Teofila feverishly tossed logs onto the fire, then for some reason stirred the water in the cauldron with a stick, as if trying to heat it faster. Then she brought a wooden washtub into the main room, filled it with steaming water, tossed in a handful of salt and a handful of sifted plum-tree ash set aside for washing – and locked the front door with two wooden bolts.

The woman's undergarments fell carelessly to the floor, her loose hair became entangled in her trembling fingers, and her skin, covered in tiny goose bumps, contracted like a snail touched by human hands.

Teofila tentatively lowered herself into the hot water – and slow, abundant tears ran down her white face. The strength and resolve inside her until recently had completely drained away. Her body resembled a straw wisp. If anyone were to have taken hold of it now, it would have fallen to pieces or snapped in half – it was so powerless and wilted. Teofila sat, her hands riveted to the edges of the washtub, like a galley-slave chained to the deck of a galley. She was only able to wriggle her toes. As if to reassure herself that she was still alive.

Then she rubbed the dry ashes over her hands. Her breasts. Her hips.

As if she was bathing for the first time in her life.

Or before her first Holy Communion.

Or before being married.

She was awaiting her death, as women expected childbirth.

She needed to be clean.

She no longer yearned after her young life. She only sobbed over it. Into the agitated bath water. Into these silent walls, which would reveal the truth to no one. She sobbed into the muted longing in her chest, which could neither be cut open with a knife nor split with an axe. The grief had become stuck fast in her swollen breasts like a leech and sucked at her – but it was unable to suck out her shame and fear.

Amid all this one single thought had never left her for a moment: she had to die clean, insomuch as her death would be horrific. Wild horses might drag her hungry female body along, tied to their hooves, and somewhere crows might peck out her glassy eyes. Then she would be unable to cover her shameful dead body, just as she had been unable to save herself from disgrace while still alive.

Teofila slowly extricated herself from the washtub. And just as she was, naked, she stood before the icon of the Holy Virgin. The water dribbled down her body and a small clear puddle grew around her, as if encircling with a wall this woman being torn asunder by fear.

What did she want to separate herself from?

From others like her?

From condemnation?

From being stoned to death?

Execution?

Teofila couldn't care less. She stood mute and frozen, her shame bared for all to see, but for the first time she was not ashamed of her nakedness.

Ever since the world and the sun had been in existence, she hadn't seen herself naked.

Especially in the middle of her own home.

In the middle of the day.

Never before had she stared at herself so diligently. She had been prevented from doing this by the shame inculcated into her from the cradle; this shame, apart from many other prescriptions and countless superstitions, dictated one especially strict and inflexible prescription for local women. A prescription which carried with it no nuances, no reservations and no mitigating circumstances: every highland woman was obliged first and foremost to be ashamed of her sex and her own body.

Always and in front of everybody.

And especially so before her wedded husband.

This law, jesuitical in nature, of forceful and constant shame was instilled in the female sex well before marriage.

Although, it should be said, it was not always adhered to.

So there was nothing strange in the fact that Hrytsko's many years of reaching his goal by groping her young body hidden under a very long nightshirt in the exceptional darkness and eerie silence had rarely awakened in Teofila any interest in his hasty nocturnal carnal actions,

135

which seemed almost premarital or villainous. In fact, on the contrary, her husband's businesslike, unhindered attainment of his goal gave birth to a morose, well-hidden disgust and a veiled resistance, both toward his dexterous and unceremonious hands, which became entangled either in her skirt or her bosom, and toward the customary coarse way in which he forced himself on her, leaving no room for tenderness or the expression of her feminine nature, even less – her desires.

Perhaps because of this long-standing resentment toward her hitherto scorned flesh, Teofila wanted to examine herself more closely. Especially before her inevitable death, in order to understand why her body, awakened only one single time, had suffered so much pain and dishonour, and now called out to her in a voice which sensed eminent demise; all the same, she felt no repentance.

Sucked out by her children, but not yet quite drooping, her breasts were staring at her wet feet, as if also lowering their eyes out of grief, shame or fear. Her full erect nipples rose and fell in time to her breathing, like the heads of forest bluebells rocking in the gusts of a morning breeze. Teofila's tight belly, cut here and there by stretch marks from the many births, would have remembered at some other time, at least for a brief moment, the sensation of hot male seed. But for now slippery reptilian fear was writhing in her loins, energized by the bathing, and her hips, covered in tiny goose bumps, were involuntarily closing up, as if defending themselves from someone's violent force.

However, even now, laced from head to foot with fear, uncertainty and languor, Teofila still felt young.

Hot.

And even at this very moment – just before her death – she yearned for that forgotten tenderness.

But the mallet of fear struck the nape of her neck for the umpteenth time – and the cowering woman slowly, but forcefully wrapped her numb arms around herself. As if imitating or recreating someone's embrace.

She stood there, her stiff palms wrapped crosswise around her body, as the last of her life force was leaving her tired body.

Just as she was, Teofila fell to her knees and passionately prayed before the icons, which also seemed to cower at the unseen audacity of the naked woman. Because suddenly, straight after finishing her prayer, she placed her palms against her barely rounded belly – and a sharp and irresistible wave of desire spread through her cold veins. And so she remained on her knees, torn asunder by the incongruous craving inside her and the rooted horror of reprisal.

Teofila raised her eyes – and the mocking, deprecating gaze of the Holy Mother of God forced the kneeling woman to do the unthinkable (even in the mind of the greatest of sinners!): she squeezed her right palm into a fist and shook it at the woman with the golden halo and doubtful immaculacy, who silently condemned Teofila from the wall, without gazing into her soul. Her trembling, but still clenched fist, held either out of despair or rage, shook before Teofila's eyes and the Holy Mother of God's. As if it intended to strike both their faces at the same time.

And slowly the hard fist began to soften, but it did not open.

And the kneeling woman continued to think that she was not the greatest female sinner in the world.

Even despite her clenched fist threatening the Holy Mother of God.

...NO MATTER HOW MUCH TEOFILA HAD WAITED for Hrytsko, no matter how much she had prepared for their meeting, when the elder son Ambrosiy blurted out the words: "Mum, dad's here!!!" just before sunset, she still felt the blood rush to her head. As if someone had struck her in the temple.

Teofila sharply tugged the lad by the arm – and remained standing that way with him in the middle of the room, like a statue of the Holy Virgin with her Son.

Covered in perspiration from the brisk walking, Hrytsko flew into the house – and stopped dead at the threshold, confronted by a strange scene.

His Teofila was standing in the middle of the room, white as snow, holding their eldest son's hand.

Draped in a loose long shirt, down to her ankles.

With her hair unbraided.

On the clay floor near her feet lay an axe, a whip and a rope used to tether cows.

A candle was burning on the table.

Up against the wall, near their bed, the old cradle was rocking slowly, tied to the beam above.

The house smelt of warmth and home cooking.

Everything was as it had been before the war.

But something was not quite right here, because why was Teofila standing almost at attention, and not throwing herself against Hrytsko's chest and not weeping with joy?

And why the axe in the middle of the room and the frayed shepherd's whip and the tethering rope?

Had the poor thing not yet grown used to the fact that the front had long since passed through here and nothing threatened them anymore?

Was the past fear stronger than the present joy?

"Filya!" Hrytsko moved from the threshold toward his wife. "Filya, I'm back from the war, fit and well, and you..." Before Keyvan had finished his thought, Teofila fell onto her knees before him and, entwining her hands around his legs, spoke for the first time:

"Kill me, Hrytsko! Cut off my head or suffocate me... but I was unable to defend myself... I couldn't defend myself, Hrytsko..." and with these words she offered him the axe.

Without a second thought, Hrytsko bounded over to the cradle like a wolf.

In the old-fashioned cradle, darkened by time, in places riddled by borers, two small children snored away. They looked to be about two years old. One of the babies, wakened by the sharp movement, suddenly blinked its sleepy eyes and began to squirm about, trying to make its way out from under the blanket. And meanwhile the second slept, as if it was in its mother's arms; it had a faint smile in the corners of its lips and quaintly moved its small eyebrows about.

Turning white as a sheet and without uttering a single word, Hrytsko ripped the cradle from its supports in a single movement and threw it on the floor with all his might.

Teofila, who had been on her knees, momentarily jumped to her feet and covered the rocking cradle on the floor with her whole body, shielding the children.

Covering his mouth with both hands, Ambrosiy hid behind the oven hearth, shrilly calling out to his father from there:

"Dad, don't kill mum… dad… don't kill her…"

The woman lay face down on the cradle and her husband beat her with iron fists.

Fiercely.

Wordlessly.

And she let his hard blows fall upon her uncovered head.

An iron hand tried to tear Teofila from the two living balls, but with arms deadlocked around the children, she only offered her head to be beaten and the insane Hrytsko tore at her loose hair, which became entwined in his fingers like river weed.

Blood ran from Teofila's mouth and nose – and she spat it out into the sleeve of her shirt, without moving her hands from the cradle.

Finally, exhausted from the beatings, Hrytsko sat on the oven hearth and dragged his eldest son toward him.

"Where are Makoviy and Khryzont? Where's Tanasiy? Prokip?" he lifted his son's chin.

"At auntie Anna's," blubbered Ambrosiy, and then buried his face in his father's chest, bursting into tears.

"Your mum's a whore – the devil take you all!" Keyvan slapped his child and came up to Teofila. "Get up! I want to know what happened!" he yanked at her torn shirt…

…TYSOVA RIVNIA HAD ALREADY silently made its peace with the third, but equally insolent arrival of an occupational army in the country, had already said prayers for the three Jews who had been killed and raked away the ashes of the houses which had been burnt down by the enemy. The village had trampled down the dust left after the plundered grain and fodder, and the people had once more bathed themselves in tears from the inflicted insults and rage, and now considered whether this third coming would be as brief as the previous two, or merely brief but invariably cruel.

The first time the Russkies had made camp in these parts for six weeks – from September till October. However, this had been enough for them to leave behind much resentment and grief.

A year later, with the front line moving hither and thither, like a farmer's wife without her husband, the Russian army managed to stay here for a whole year and a bit more.

And so when in June 1916 the foreigners arrived in Tysova Rivnia for a third time, even the children ran headlong to avoid them.

...TEOFILA AND HER SISTER Anna were earthing up the potatoes in the garden, while her three older boys, Ambrosiy, Makoviy and Khryzont, were grazing the cows nearby. The smaller Tanasiy and Prokip were playing alongside them, when suddenly dust began to rise in a cloud from the habitually silent village road, raised by the hooves of countless horses, and the surrounding stillness came alive with the gibberish of foreign voices.

Keyvan's wife knew that the enemy had entered the village along this road twice before.

"Again!" yelled Teofila, and threw her hoe down among the rows of potato plants, painfully yanking Anna's bared elbow. "Let's hide in the cellar," she herded the frightened children. "Only hurry up!"

By the time the seven of them had reached their yard, two soldiers were already standing there watering their horses.

"Oh!" one of them clapped his hands, seeing the frightened women who were short of breath. "Oh! You!" he smiled avidly and beckoned to Anna with his finger.

He was young. Probably the same age as Teofila. Black, like black tar covered in dust. Thick curly hair struggled out from under the light Kuban Cossack hat on his head, and his thin waist was girded by a wide leather belt sitting atop a dark-blue woolen cloth uniform without buttons, resembling a wraparound coat or a felt cloak. The ends were wrapped over each other. From under this strange attire peered a dark shirt and similar pants. At the black soldier's side hung a sheathed sabre. And he stood rocking from his heels to his toes, as if choosing a rhythm to the conversation.

"You!" the soldier approached the women, continuing to point his finger at Anna. "Give water. I wanting water," the black man jabbered, using one hand to push aside Teofila's arm, with which she was shielding her sister, and meanwhile keeping the other on his sabre. "You!" he mirthfully threatened Teofila with his index finger. "She give me water," he pointed at Anna a second time, having first run his eyes over Teofila.

Anna, white as cherry blossom, was trembling behind her older sister, trying to hide her breasts. Her tanned arms were trembling too – and all this made her look like a frightened bird.

"Your husband?" the soldier asked Teofila, pointing to each of the boys who had grabbed hold of their mother's skirt with both hands.

"My children! Children. These are my children. And this is my sister," Teofila replied feverishly, grabbing hold of the well crank. "I'll get you some water myself. Just a moment," she grabbed hold of the swinging bucket with her trembling hands.

142

"You!" the soldier pointed his finger at Anna once more. "You... give water."

Deathly scared, Anna slowly moved her sister aside and, trembling, bent over the well joist to grab hold of the bucket.

And at this moment the black man slapped Anna's backside from behind, then turned her around with both arms to face him and rested his hand on her bosom.

"Don't touch her!" Teofila forgot herself and struck the foreigner in the chest with the back of her hand, and then let him have it in the face: "Leave her alone! She's expecting her lad from the war," she fell to her knees before him. "Anna, run away, Anna! Run away with the children!" she yelled at her sister, while she herself grabbed hold of the foreigner by the skirt of his strange uniform and struck her head against his knees: "Don't touch her! She's a virgin!"

The soldier only smiled strangely, as if not noticing Teofila's slaps. He jabbered something in his own language to his partner and the fellow, placing his finger to his lips, told both of the women to remain silent. Spreading his arms wide apart, he made his way toward Anna and the children, as if intending to embrace them.

With the frightened boys pressed up against her, Anna stood stock-still beside the well, continuing to cover her breasts with her hands. Tears rolled down her face, but she did not wipe them away. And the soldier advancing with his arms spread apart, suddenly straightened and dropped his arms to his side, as if preparing to salute Anna and the children.

He put his finger to his lips again.

And then he looked around. His comrade, having taken hold of Teofila's plait, which had slipped out from under her kerchief, had wound it round his hand like the thong of a whip, and was pushing the older sister through the door of the barn, which was slightly ajar. She was holding onto both his dusty boots, and it was hard to say whether she was defending herself or assisting him.

…What happened next, Teofila tried not to admit even to herself.

Because as soon as the hinges of the door had creaked shut behind them and the barn became filled with semi-darkness, the foreign black rapist became an ordinary man, just as thirsty for affection as Teofila in her nocturnal dreams, after spending several years apart from Hrytsko. She would never have thought that the first random male hand – a stranger's male hand! – could have so easily stung her secret spot, previously inaccessible to strangers and that it could have so swiftly destroyed what she had always thought to be her rockhard female will.

For the first few minutes, the Circassian snarled like a hungry male, ready to tear the female to pieces.

And in exactly the same way the suddenly captive female first resembled a wounded bitch: she writhed from the pain and howled in despair, scratched at his face and bit his skin, kicked the attacker with her feet, attempted to free herself from his frantic embrace.

But he only sniffed at her and pressed her closer with the pincers of his arms.

Perhaps it would have ended like that, with the man and the woman (both equally insane: he from passion, she from fear) conquering each other and they would have jumped apart forever, had that stupid linen skirt draped over her linen shirt not been pushed up above

Teofila's knee in this uneven contest, exposing her white legs – so white, as if she had lived in a cellar.

At that moment the Circassian's arms suddenly unlocked and his right palm, hot as a glowing coal, first rested on her inner thigh, and then slowly, but boldly made its way up.

It was so tender, so deathly fiery and gentle, so impossibly delicious and invocatory, that Teofila's legs could not bear such torture: they unlocked themselves before this male force and were now reduced to submission.

There was no thought... no fear... only a strange white crucifix glimmered inside her head, as if in a mist. Because that damned Circassian, with eyes as black as the earth, embedded his gaze into her eyes and with one hand caressed her hips, while the other fingered her resilient breasts. His lips, his warm meaty lips, sucked the last juices from her lips, as if looking for honey, or perhaps, on the contrary, pouring honey into Teofila...

And with her entire body awakened, she pressed forward toward him. And so brazenly, so compliantly and ardently, that even the Circassian broke away from her for a moment in surprise, but then fell with a shudder upon her lap, trembling and moist, as if freshly bathed.

...Afterwards Teofila would sometimes stare at the small trampled pile of hay in the corner of the barn, where she had so easily been tamed, but not crushed, no, not crushed, only her feminine honour had been tarnished. And each time a mixture of fear, and awe, and lethargy filled her chest.

Had the roof caved in then, or had the earth parted, had a knife become imbedded in her throat or a bullet been fired into her heart, she would have accepted this far more easily, than having now to accept the thought that as a result of one single moment of a barbarous

145

struggle and brief submission she had received such an ecstatic and hitherto unknown moment of pleasure. In that single instant of utter exultation her unawakened body had felt something.

Because afterwards, after everything was over, her previously limp hand again forcefully slapped the attacker across his face: until now only her husband had known how white her body was. And now a stranger knew as well!

But in reply the soldier softly and gratefully rubbed his face against her arm and then fell back on the hay, as if wanting to rest.

At that moment she could have smashed the Circassian's head in: while there were no weapons in the barn, there were plenty of sickles, scythes, axes, spades and pitchforks resting an arm's length away.

However, the satiated woman did not care to stretch out her weakened arm…

And when she realized that she had become pregnant, she had wanted to drown herself. But the river was tiny, and her children even tinier. She tried to poison the black seed inside her with herbs… and jumped off the stable roof… lifted heavy loads… but her tight belly became more and more rounded.

However, when Teofila felt the baby inside her, she gave in to God's will. She would not be the first in this predicament in their village, nor the last. And she was not to blame that God and the Kaiser had taken her husband off to war and left her at the mercy of fate.

So had the Lord Himself not wanted her to be pregnant again?

Had He not sent her the black man?

Had He not poured his black seed into her?

For nothing happened in this or the other world without God's will!

She knew that. That's what she had been taught.

So who, then, could rebuke her, if the Lord's finger had rested upon her?

...After two children had emerged into the world from her loins, she didn't even look in their direction for a whole day, didn't even ask who she had given birth to and did not give them her breast to suckle. She only knew that there were two of them. And that they had arms and legs.

She waited for them to die.

From infantile diarrhea.

Or whatever other illness would take them.

The old local midwife Marfa whispered something with her toothless mouth over the cradle and gave the infants herbal teas, but did not force Teofila to breast-feed them. She only glanced silently at her, for she knew: people weren't like dung, they would eventually soften. And Keyvan's wife would loosen up. Only not immediately. The children weren't to blame. Neither was Teofila. Only the war and the Kaiser had to be cursed.

...Meanwhile Teofila kept her eyes fixed on the village high road, where the dust rose in a cloud many a time under the hooves of strangers' horses. But the horses bearing black people did not return.

Neither did Hrytsko.

And so she laid out the smallest boys – the two of them together – on both sides of her breasts overflowing with milk. Like lively puppies, the infants fixed their puffy lips on her teats, and her unvoiced hostility toward the living bundles slowly dissolved away. In its place fear began to grow beneath her breasts. But for the moment Teofila took no notice of it. Whatever would be, would be. When she was nursing her black boys, a semi-conscious languid feeling spread from her breasts to her loins and her eyes grew misty. So that she was ready to grab the sleeve of any passer-by, stare into his eyes and ask if he had seen the black man anywhere? Had the fellow asked for news of her? Was he longing after her aroused body...?

And the two infant boys smacked their lips and sweetly wheezed as they suckled. Teofila dripped tears upon their white faces – and did not wipe them away.

... SO THAT WHEN IVAN VARVARCHUK asked Hrytsko to help him with some men's business, Keyvan was not very surprised.

At first he felt somewhat frightened by the request.

Righteous Lord!

How?

How could he go and help someone kill his godson Dmytryk?

How could he raise a hand to beat an innocent lad?

Dmytryk was innocent – Hrytsko was sure of that.

Men were never guilty. It was all female will. Their spells and wiles. The devilish attraction of their exposed bodies. The sudden lightning bolt of their glance. And their smell. The enticing smell of a ripe woman's loins, which weakened a man's resolve and steadfastness. And nothing else.

If Teofila had not been so shapely... had she had washed-out eyes and dried-up breasts... had she defended herself, instead of spreading her legs...

Would that Circassian have left his foul black seed inside her?

Would those detestable children have hatched from Teofila's womb?!

Hrytsko had not raped any strange women while at war, even if they had laid themselves out before him! He had taken them – because they themselves had wanted this, and he desperately needed to do it. To maintain his health. But to rape women – the Lord forbid.

...Varvarchuk was saying something.

Meanwhile Keyvan was thinking.

And then he felt a sense of relief. Yes-yes. Keyvan felt the dormant rage awaken inside him. He had continually smothered it, because he had no other option.

What else could he do?

Were he to kill his wife, he would have had to feed seven children.

And who would feed them, if he were thrown into prison?

Smother the two black bastards...

He could not raise his hand against them after his five children (yes, his children!), surrounded the tiny little Circassians, defending them from their father's rage. And the eldest, Ambrosiy, grabbed both his arms:

"Kill us all with them, dad, because we're all brothers. And we have one mum."

Hrytsko's resolve cracked then, like a dry branch.

He had not been a rapist, and he would not become a child killer.

But what was he to do, if people laughed at him silently?

Maybe they didn't? For after the war, every house had its own bitter pill.

With his revenge against Dmytryk, Varvarchuk had saved Hrytsko. Rescued him, as if he had pulled a drowned man out of the water... as if he had brought a hanged man back to life. Otherwise Hrytsko would have gone insane.

Oh, yes. Ivan was certain that Keyvan was helping him remove the soul from Dmytryk's body. But it was not so.

It wasn't Dmytryk that Hrytsko's strong feet trampled between the boards. No, not Dmytryk at all. Keyvan was squashing to death the Circassian, jumping on him with the soles of his feet. He was killing the black Circassian and his two hatchlings from Teofila's womb. He was releasing his fierce rage and internal unextinguished fire. It was his dark revenge. He had killed his subdued hatred back there in Varvarchuk's house.

And what was the result?! Dear little righteous Lord... Lord, what an abyss that black revenge had dragged him into! Hrytsko's life had rolled along the road of fear away from his rage. And now it was sealed completely. Another month or two, and Keyvan would be wishing this world goodbye. Supposedly kind, but in actual fact a tormented man more fierce than an animal, he had smeared his lips with lies until this day. Until he had spilled the truth to Odokiyka, Cheviuk's eldest daughter-in-law. And what had been the result of that truth? Zilch! Because while Hrytsko lived with his secret, he bore the hope that liberation from it would bring him release. That it would remove the heavy burden from his soul. But the secret about Dmytryk turned out to be an empty one. Keyvan's secret turned out to be wretched – it had never even been a secret for Cheviuk's Odokiya.

HRYTSKO CLOSED HIS EYES – and immediately somewhere from the black darkness emerged the smiling face of a much younger Kyrylo Cheviuk. Kind Kyrylo, with arms extended, seemed to be floating toward Hrytsko. As if wanting to embrace him and slap him on the shoulders, as he loved to do with everyone whom he met on the road. 'Dear mister comrade!' Kyrylo would call out to approaching people, both young and old, as his frank smile stretched from ear to ear. 'How's your day been? Everything all right?'

White as a sheet even in his dreams, Keyvan drew back from the spectre and with all his might tried to beat it off with his arms, sliding to the floor and striking his head against the bed. God! How long would this torment last? Had he even thought about Kyrylo's death when he had gone off to the Jewish lawyer to bear witness, masquerading as old Cheviuk, in order to falsely rewrite the will to benefit Oksentiy instead of Pavlo?! Even then Hrytsko thought only of his resentment toward Teofila and suppressed his hatred toward the two children, who looked at him with a foreigner's eyes, black as coal, but spoke to him in his own language...

He beat Teofila whenever he could, as if she were a stray dog who had stolen the best leg of ham from the house.

"Make sure that I have to look for you!" Hrytsko told his wife each morning, as soon as he opened his eyes.

And, bent double, she would disappear for days on end, either in the garden or the stable. She even took out the kitchen utensils into the summer kitchen, where they usually cooked swill for the pigs.

"Lord, give the chicken some brains!" Hrytsko admonished the morose Teofila for the slightest trifle, at any opportunity, in any company.

However he slept with her all the same and did not raise his hand against the children that were not his.

But that did not extinguish the fire in his chest.

...MUTE, OR OLEKSA HOVDIA AS HE WAS ALSO KNOWN, stopped in the orchard under Marynka-God-spirit's pear tree practically in the middle of the night. A time when people and roosters were fast asleep. And dogs and thieves were too lazy to get about.

Hovdia first moved about the orchard barefoot and on tip-toe.

The orchard wasn't yet glistening with dew, although the grass was cold with moisture. The overgrown trees, neglected for a long time, hung sullenly over the earth, the black cudgels of their branches drooping to the ground; and only the young cherry trees rustled, their rounded white crowns pushing into the sky.

For a long time Mute caressed the moist trunks. He looked under the prickly bushes of gooseberry.

Then he stood for even longer under the pear tree to which Marynka's swing was tied.

Oleksa pushed the swing gently, and the swing creaked like an unoiled house door.

Hovdia stopped the swing with his hand. He knew about Marynka's age-old habit of sitting on this swing – and then telling a person all about their life.

But a single nagging old thought would not let Oleksa sleep to this day: why hadn't the god-spirited old maid Marynka warned him not to go hunting with Kyrylo?!

Wouldn't he have listened to her? He sooner would have disobeyed Kyrylo and his sons, rather than go against Marynka's advice, for he knew that her information came from the other side. Marynka's voices were like Oleksa's keen smell. For some reason his nose had brought him here to the orchard and the swing on this night.

For some reason?!

Oh, no. Not for *some* reason!

Not for *some* reason: Kyrylo's scent had again brought Oleksa to Marynka's orchard.

God in Heaven! Kyrylo's burnt bones must have already turned to dust in the earth, having fertilized the grass and the trees in the cemetery, but Oleksa could still smell Kyrylo's scent in Marynka's orchard. Right here, under the swing.

Hovdia sat on the swing, holding the frayed ropes, supporting Marynka's plaything with both hands. He did not swing himself. Only took a deep breath of the sharp midnight air and thought.

His nose had brought him here, together with distant and forgotten voices. Something had brought him here on this night to this almost wild orchard and to this swing, where forgotten voices had become discernible. If Hovdia had been able to speak, he would have scratched at old Marynka's window and would have asked her what she had going with Kyrylo? Or at the very least he would have asked her why he, Mute, had to bear the brunt of the sin of Kyrylo Cheviuk's death, a man who had been the kindest person in the world to him? And why was his smell still here?

Oleksa pummeled his head with his fists, as if he were bashing walnuts off a tree. He felt that if he didn't do this – a black pestilence would throw him against the ground. Then he would forget why his nose had brought him here. And it had brought him here for some reason. After so many years... of sleepless nights... of horrors... of wordless sobbing.

If back then, in the hut on Ivantsio's Field, while cleaning his rifle, Oleksa had not been thinking about Marynka, having suddenly sensed her smell there, her white shadow mightn't have appeared against the wall of the hut then, exactly where Kyrylo was standing preparing dinner.

But what a shadow it had been! White, weightless, like a small summer cloud... for some reason it did not float toward Oleksa, but hovered over Kyrylo, as if greatly overjoyed, and all but spread-eagled itself before his agile male body.

Oleksa had felt a sharp pain in his heart and felt as if the butt-end of an axe had struck his head: it couldn't be! Impossible! Kyrylo had a throng of children and grandchildren. Kyrylo never even turned his head to look at another woman, having eyes only for his own wife. And here the god-spirited old spinster was spreading herself out before him, like grass mown with a scythe?!

Had Oleksa shot at Kyrylo then, instead of at Marynka's apparition hovering above his rival's head?!

How else could he have appeased or extinguished the jealousy inside him at that moment?!

Was it Oleksa's fault that, having returned from the war, he had wanted that god-spirited older woman so much, like a child wanting its mother's breast milk? Hovdia had wanted someone like himself, not simply Marynka!

Had Kyrylo's Vasylyna been the same, he probably would have craved her. However, back then his nose had pointed him in the direction of Marynka – and no one else.

But how could he have desired this pious woman? She was almost old enough to be his mother, while he himself was old enough to be Kyrylo's son?

Those first years Hovdia walked in bewilderment along the streets near Marynka's place.

For nights on end he stood outside her house, tormenting his soul with doubts about whether some male hand might be scratching at her door.

He would stop at a distance and watch her speaking to people or pottering about in her yard.

He would stop her in the street or on forest paths to give her apples or berries.

One time, having come across her near the river, he unexpectedly stroked her head with his rough hand and looked her straight in the eye, sensing a sudden flash of lightning strike down his male strength.

Marynka suddenly turned white but did not pull back or slap him. She only closed one eye. Smiled to herself. And wordlessly took the hand which had stroked her between her two hands. And held it, barely moving her fingers against his. "Stop the passion, Oleksa..." she said, clearing her throat. "The heart is a stupid business. Forget about it. Blink your way through it or sob it all out. But our joy is not to be..."

And she walked off along the riverbank, never once looking back.

He had roared painfully then, like a bull tethered for the first time with a ring in its nostrils. Oleksa fell to the ground, ripped out tufts of grass, and would have been prepared to chew on them, if only he could feel Marynka's gentle hand upon his own once more, stroking him through his shirt, as no one had ever stroked him before. He had wanted to pursue Marynka's disappearing figure, to dig his fingernails into her shoulders, and to shake her, embrace her, until she fainted in his arms; he would have at last sated his hungry soul, smelling her all over, from

155

head to foot, and brushing his lips across her face. Oleksa wouldn't have wanted any more from her: only to be able to hold her in his arms and breath in her smells, like one intoxicated, with the knowledge that only he could do this with her.

But here, God Almighty... sinless Marynka was circling in a shadow above Kyrylo's shoulders without the slightest shame, as if wanting to rest against his bare chest.

Back then in that hut on Ivantsio's Field a sinister jealousy and fury had exploded within Oleksa and made him press the trigger of the unpolished rifle aimed at the white cloud surrounding Cheviuk.

Obviously it must have been that. Blinding, furious jealousy. Because Mute remained silent, and Kyrylo kept slicing salted meat and moving his lips. And the forever dark Marynka noiselessly bent over Kyrylo in her white clothing, her lips smiling.

How could such a thing be happening before his eyes?!

Oleksa had only wanted to drive away the apparition.

Because no one had the right to touch Marynka.

Not even his kindest and best master, Kyrylo.

... Hovdia did not remain for long on Marynka's swing. The distant, long-forgotten smell of Kyrylo was coming up through the grass under the swing... or drifting across from the sleepy house, where the god-spirited woman was finishing her dreams. Even now, wrinkled and hunched over, black as the earth, she still made the ageing Oleksa Mute feel uneasy.

And he shrugged his shoulders.

Either out of astonishment or rage: even after his death Kyrylo had not left Oleksa in peace.

Or perhaps he had not forgiven him? Because why else would Kyrylo's soul still be in Marynka's orchard?!

But Hovdia's anger did not last long. Only until the neighbour's rooster had found its voice.

After that Oleksa stopped thinking. He jumped to his feet, pulled a knife from his pants, hacked at the rope, and then deftly, like a young lad, bounded over the leaning fence.

...MARYNKA WAS FOUND just before noon by Petrunia Varvarchuk, when she brought her some milk. Spread-eagled under the pear tree, the woman lay with her chest upon the smashed swing, her stiff arms embracing the slashed rope. From the pocket of her black goatskin *keptar* peered a wax candle braided into a plait, which people in the mountains reserved for the dead.

Petrunia slowly bent over Marynka, as if intending to whisper something into her ear, so as not to scare her. But suddenly she pulled away sharply:

Marynka's body exuded a man's smell,
a mix of trampled grass and salty sweat,
ripe apples and fresh milk,
the skin of a young lamb
and the smell of Dmytryk's slippery seed, which he had
once spilled on Petrunia's white hips.
The smell was so fresh, sharp and familiar, that Petrunia
became startled, crossing herself with both
hands at once. She backed off into the depths
of the orchard, and then yelled at the top of
her voice, for the whole village to hear,

157

with the voice of a turtledove
ounded in the throat.
Or perhaps in the heart...

9 October 2006 – 25 February 2007,
Kyiv – Mykulychyn in Ivano-Frankivsk Province – Kyiv

Dear Reader,

Thank you for purchasing this book.

We at Glagoslav Publications are glad to welcome you, and hope that you find our books to be a source of knowledge and inspiration.

We want to show the beauty and depth of the Slavic region to everyone looking to expand their horizon and learn something new about different cultures, different people, and we believe that with this book we have managed to do just that.

Now that you've got to know us, we want to get to know you. We value communication with our readers and want to hear from you! We offer several options:

— Join our Book Club on Goodreads, Library Thing and Shelfari, and receive special offers and information about our giveaways;

— Share your opinion about our books on Amazon, Barnes & Noble, Waterstones and other bookstores;

— Join us on Facebook and Twitter for updates on our publications and news about our authors;

— Visit our site www.glagoslav.com to check out our Catalogue and subscribe to our Newsletter.

Glagoslav Publications is getting ready to release a new collection and planning some interesting surprises — stay with us to find out!

Glagoslav Publications
Email: contact@glagoslav.com

Glagoslav Publications Catalogue

- *A History of Belarus* by Lubov Bazan
- *Children's Fashion of the Russian Empire* by Alexander Vasiliev
- *Empire of Corruption: The Russian National Pastime* by Vladimir Soloviev
- *Heroes of the 90s: People and Money. The Modern History of Russian Capitalism* by Alexander Solovev, Vladislav Dorofeev and Valeria Bashkirova
- *Fifty Highlights from the Russian Literature* (Dutch Edition) by Maarten Tengbergen
- *Bajesvolk* (Dutch Edition) by Michail Chodorkovsky
- *Dagboek van Keizerin Alexandra* (Dutch Edition)
- *Myths about Russia* by Vladimir Medinskiy
- *Boris Yeltsin: The Decade that Shook the World* by Boris Minaev
- *A Man Of Change: A study of the political life of Boris Yeltsin*
- *Sberbank: The Rebirth of Russia's Financial Giant* by Evgeny Karasyuk
- *To Get Ukraine* by Oleksandr Shyshko
- *Asystole* by Oleg Pavlov
- *Gnedich* by Maria Rybakova
- *Marina Tsvetaeva: The Essential Poetry*
- *Multiple Personalities* by Tatyana Shcherbina
- *The Investigator* by Margarita Khemlin
- *The Exile* by Zinaida Tulub
- *Leo Tolstoy: Flight from Paradise* by Pavel Basinsky
- *Moscow in the 1930* by Natalia Gromova
- *Laurus* (Dutch edition) by Evgenij Vodolazkin
- *Prisoner* by Anna Nemzer
- *The Crime of Chernobyl: The Nuclear Goulag* by Wladimir Tchertkoff
- *Alpine Ballad* by Vasil Bykau
- *The Complete Correspondence of Hryhory Skovoroda*
- *The Tale of Aypi* by Ak Welsapar
- *Selected Poems* by Lydia Grigorieva
- *The Fantastic Worlds of Yuri Vynnychuk*
- *The Garden of Divine Songs and Collected Poetry of Hryhory Skovoroda*
- *Adventures in the Slavic Kitchen: A Book of Essays with Recipes* by Igor Klekh
- *Seven Signs of the Lion* by Michael M. Naydan

- *Forefathers' Eve* by Adam Mickiewicz
- *One-Two* by Igor Eliseev
- *Girls, be Good* by Bojan Babić
- *Time of the Octopus* by Anatoly Kucherena
- *The Grand Harmony* by Bohdan Ihor Antonych
- *The Selected Lyric Poetry Of Maksym Rylsky*
- *The Shining Light* by Galymkair Mutanov
- *The Frontier: 28 Contemporary Ukrainian Poets - An Anthology*
- *Acropolis: The Wawel Plays* by Stanisław Wyspiański
- *Contours of the City* by Attyla Mohylny
- *Conversations Before Silence: The Selected Poetry of Oles Ilchenko*
- *The Secret History of my Sojourn in Russia* by Jaroslav Hašek
- *Mirror Sand: An Anthology of Russian Short Poems*
- *Maybe We're Leaving* by Jan Balaban
- *Death of the Snake Catcher* by Ak Welsapar
- *A Brown Man in Russia* by Vijay Menon
- *Hard Times* by Ostap Vyshnia
- *The Flying Dutchman* by Anatoly Kudryavitsky
- *Nikolai Gumilev's Africa* by Nikolai Gumilev
- *Combustions* by Srđan Srdić
- *The Sonnets* by Adam Mickiewicz
- *Dramatic Works* by Zygmunt Krasiński
- *Four Plays* by Juliusz Słowacki
- *Little Zinnobers* by Elena Chizhova
- *We Are Building Capitalism! Moscow in Transition 1992-1997* by Robert Stephenson
- *The Nuremberg Trials* by Alexander Zvyagintsev
- *The Hemingway Game* by Evgeni Grishkovets
- *A Flame Out at Sea* by Dmitry Novikov
- *Jesus' Cat* by Grig
- *Want a Baby and Other Plays* by Sergei Tretyakov
- *Mikhail Bulgakov: The Life and Times* by Marietta Chudakova
- *Leonardo's Handwriting* by Dina Rubina
- *A Burglar of the Better Sort* by Tytus Czyżewski
- *The Mouseiad and other Mock Epics* by Ignacy Krasicki

- *Ravens before Noah* by Susanna Harutyunyan
- *An English Queen and Stalingrad* by Natalia Kulishenko
- *Point Zero* by Narek Malian
- *Absolute Zero* by Artem Chekh
- *Olanda* by Rafał Wojasiński
- *Robinsons* by Aram Pachyan
- *The Monastery* by Zakhar Prilepin
- *The Selected Poetry of Bohdan Rubchak: Songs of Love, Songs of Death, Songs of the Moon*
- *Mebet* by Alexander Grigorenko
- *The Orchestra* by Vladimir Gonik
- *Everyday Stories* by Mima Mihajlović
- *Slavdom* by Ľudovít Štúr
- *The Code of Civilization* by Vyacheslav Nikonov
- *Where Was the Angel Going?* by Jan Balaban
- *De Zwarte Kip* (Dutch Edition) by Antoni Pogorelski
- *Głosy / Voices* by Jan Polkowski
- *Sergei Tretyakov: A Revolutionary Writer in Stalin's Russia* by Robert Leach
- *Opstand* (Dutch Edition) by Władysław Reymont
- *Dramatic Works* by Cyprian Kamil Norwid
- *Children's First Book of Chess* by Natalie Shevando and Matthew McMillion
- *The Revolt of the Animals* by Wladyslaw Reymont
- *Illegal Parnassus* by Bojan Babić
- *Liza's Waterfall: The hidden story of a Russian feminist* by Pavel Basinsky
- *Precursor* by Vasyl Shevchuk
- *The Vow: A Requiem for the Fifties* by Jiří Kratochvil
- *Duel* by Borys Antonenko-Davydovych
- *Subterranean Fire* by Natalka Bilotserkivets
- *Biography of Sergei Prokofiev* by Igor Vishnevetsky

More coming . . .

Printed in the USA
CPSIA information can be obtained
at www.ICGtesting.com
LVHW090314181223
766737LV00009B/438